Feels Too Good To Be Bad

BLOOD MONEY BILLIONAIRE
BOOK FOUR

BLAIR BUTLER

FIRE FINCH

CHAPTER 1
Inky Dream

IVY

A young blonde woman stands on the deck in the dark. Blunt-cut bobbed hair, supermodel figure, sophisticated pantsuit the same color as the night sky. She oozes money and authority, and she sparkles with violence.

"Anya," says Alistair. It's a guttural sound edged with pure fear.

The woman dips her chin in accordance.

All the softness leaves my body.

Anya? Who the fuck—?

Alistair's fingers wrap around my wrist so hard it hurts.

He looks into my eyes for just a second. "Ivy. Forgive me."

Before I can ask him what he means, he sweeps me off my feet. Confused, I think he's going to carry me, but then my body keeps traveling in the air, and that's when he lets go.

Alistair fucking lets me go over the yacht's railing.

I'm twirling in the dark space for a moment that feels like forever.

I hit the black water with a gasp that almost drowns me. The cold is shocking, but nothing is more horrifying than the fact that it was Alistair who threw me overboard.

I'm gasping and spluttering, legs kicking, arms waving. I see the twinkling lights of the yacht and hear the music. No one knows I'm in the black water apart from Alistair and the strange woman he called Anya. Fuck! I'm in shock. I need to hold it together. I scream as loudly as I can.

"Help!" I yell, but my voice isn't loud enough. I'm choking on the seawater and using the limited breath I have to stay afloat.

I try again. "HELP! Help me!"

My cries only make me feel more isolated, more in peril. No one will hear me over the music and laughter of the party on board. I try one more time, hoping for a miracle, because if I don't get back on the yacht I'm as good as dead. Dry land is miles away. I'm about to shout again when I see her. She's at the railing, looking down at me. I know she's the enemy, I can feel it deep in my body, but that same body screams for her help because she's the only one who can save me.

"Please!" I sob, in between long shuddering gasps for breath. Salty water droplets find their way into my mouth. I spit them out. "Please!"

I'm searching her face for any kind of mercy. She's far up, and I'm flailing, so I can't see much, but there is certainly no compassion in her expression. I give one last cry, knowing that if she doesn't call the crew now, I'll drown waiting for help. Her face is an ice sculpture.

I realize I'll have to swim back to shore if I want any chance of survival. I'm not confident I'll make it, but it's my only hope. I look up at Anya, begging her with my snotty sobbing. She raises her gun and aims it at me.

No! My heart smashes against my ribs.

Her first shot misses me by a hair, and I scream. I can't help it; the sounds just tears out of my throat. The party music and the gun's silencer mean no one hears it. Anya takes aim again, and I know this time she won't miss. I haul in a shaky breath and go underwater, moving as quickly as I can away from the water I'd just been treading. I see and hear the bullet torpedo the water barely an inch away from me. I stay under as long as I can, but the adrenaline pushes me up for air.

She's about to take her third shot when I see Alistair slam into her. His face is a mask of outright fury. She yells in surprise and frustration as her gun tumbles out of her hand and plops into the ocean. I yelp in relief. Alistair has disarmed her, so I'm sure he'll be able to help me back on board. Perhaps I won't die tonight after all.

Anya yells and tries to attack Alistair, but he's too quick and too strong for her. He temporarily immobilizes her with a blow to the stomach. *Yes!* I'm so relieved that I almost sink, forgetting that I still need to kick to stay above the water. Of course he'll save me. It's Alistair! Alistair would rather die than see me suffer. Anya launches herself at him again, but he easily deflects her blows. *We're going to be okay,* I tell myself. *We're going to be okay.*

A string of fairy lights sway. Someone else is there. A man in black appears behind Alistair, camouflaged by the night sky.

"Behind you!" I scream.

He spins around, ready to fight. But the man in black didn't come here to fight. He lifts his gun.

A silenced gunshot, then another in quick succession. Two small pops, and Alistair keels over.

A blood-curdling scream so loud and horrified rises from me. It's an animalistic sound I've never heard before. Pure anguish, pure pain, and incomprehensible grief scour my lungs and throat, delivering the guttural moan of desolation.

"No" is the only word that I'm capable of thinking. *No, no, no.*

This is not real. It's an awful dream. This is not happening. Soon I'll wake up in Alistair's arms in his beautiful home, the sun streaming in the window, Reacher and Bijou basking in the rays. Safe and dry and warm. Brumilde will be frying pancakes in the kitchen. I'll clasp at my heart and say, "Oh my god. I've just had the most terrifying night-mare," and Alistair will pull me in close and kiss my neck, all warm skin and muscle. And he'll say, "It's over now. You're safe."

Not this. Not this insane surreal moment, not a fake honeymoon in Thailand. Not a psychotic blonde stranger and her black-clad shadow who wants us dead. It's just an ugly dream that I need to wake up from. I'm shaking so hard my teeth chatter in between my sobbing.

Wake up, I whisper to myself, *wake up.* My vocal cords feel shredded. My legs begin to run out of energy. I don't have to kick any longer, because this is a dream. If I just relax into the dark water I'll wake up on the other side, warm and safe. Alistair's heart will be beating, strong and steady.

So I stop weeping.

I stop kicking.

And I let the inky dream take me.

CHAPTER 2

Revenge Doesn't Pay Dividends

ALISTAIR

I wake up with a jolt as if someone has jammed a Taser in my chest. My ribcage is on fire. My eyes fly open as I drag in a long, labored breath.

I'm alone.

An assault of fresh memories and confused thoughts enter my mind.

Ivy.

I scrunch my eyes shut, willing to go back in time. Back to when Ivy was safe and happy. Instead of ... what? Drowning? Dead?

My whole body contorts violently at the thought. No way. No chance she's dead.

I would never allow that to happen.

I threw Ivy overboard because the second I looked into Anya Kuznetsov's eyes I knew she had come to murder Ivy. She may have planned to kill me, too, but I didn't care about that. She wanted to hurt me in the worst way possible, and she knew that Ivy was the ticket. I didn't stop to think. I knew instinctively that I had to remove Ivy from the situation. I hate that she had to land in the ocean, but it was the only way to keep her safe. It was the only thing I could do. God, I hate myself.

I'm outside. Not on the yacht. There is solid ground beneath me. Why didn't they just toss my body overboard? Now they're going to have to deal with a ninety-two-kilogram corpse. It's hard work—I know from experience because you can't always call the cleaners—so I guess I get the last laugh. I get to die smug.

No.

My breath catches in my throat.

Ivy.

She's okay, I tell myself. She's strong and brave. She'll make it to the shore.

Unless one of those bullets caught her.

No. She yelled that warning at me after Anya's shots were fired. She didn't take a bullet. She'll be fine.

Pain cascades through my body, and I can't tell if it's physical or emotional. I'm the reason Ivy's life's in danger. That is unforgivable. My heart aches with the pain and fury of it. My body hums with guilt and shame. What kind of man can't protect his woman? Or, worse, what kind of man put his woman in danger in the first place?

I groan, moving my head from side to side to try to escape the pain.

What have I done?

All I see is Ivy's face, her beautiful open expression, her eyes lit up by her generous smile. If she is dead, I will die, too. I refuse to exist in a world that she no longer lives in.

This deal I make with myself helps with the agony. There will be a way out of the all-consuming grief. I won't have to deal with it for too long.

As I start feeling comforted by this, I think of baby Alex. I think of Mariya.

A new dagger of sorrow is plunged deep in my chest, because I know that I can't leave Alex an orphan again. No matter how much pain I'm in, I'll have to keep going.

I grunt in despair. There will be no way out of this all-consuming pain. I will have to bear the unbearable.

I gasp as a new acute pain stings my lower side ribs. The agony sparkles down my spine. I open my eyes to see Anya looking down at me as if I am a cockroach. She had kicked me with her pointy designer shoes, and now one is placed on my breastbone.

"Ravenscroft," she drawls in her rich Moscovian accent.

"Why am I still alive?" I croak.

Her hair falls forward as she smirks down at me. "Because I have not yet given my permission for you to die."

"Ah," I reply. "So ... shooting me twice in the chest doesn't count as permission to die?"

She snorts. "Oh, please. Two baby bullets? They're just little mosquito bites."

So that's why I'm still alive. Non-lethal ammo. Mosquitos that break your ribs.

Anya reads my thoughts. "Arkadi knew it was imperative to keep you alive. He's a brilliant marksman. A little enthusiastic, perhaps, but an excellent shot."

"Your bodyguard," I guess.

Anya nods. "Amongst other things."

"So, you wanted me alive," I say. Hence the fact that I'm not currently lying on the ocean floor, being torn apart by serrated-jawed fish.

Anya smiles. Her eyes have an evil twinkle. "Of course I want you alive. What use to me would you be if you weren't breathing?"

Her spiky heel is digging into my breastbone, and the pressure from the rest of her shoe is ramping up the burning ache in my ribs. It's getting harder to catch my breath.

"I thought you'd kill me. And the rest of my family. Revenge."

"That would be extremely shortsighted, don't you think? Revenge doesn't pay dividends."

"So it's dividends you're after?"

"In a manner of speaking, yes."

She presses harder, and I start seeing stars. I may have lost some blood: I feel light, as if I could float above my damaged body. Maybe I will die without Anya Kuznetsov's permission, after all.

CHAPTER 3
Ebony Razor

IVY

It's a good feeling, to just let go. To let the water take me inside and out. It's a relief to sink slowly into the depths of the ocean. It feels like I'm traveling toward the center of the universe. No rush, no light, no pain. My whole body relaxes. I can't tell if the water is warm or cold; my skin no longer senses the difference. Or perhaps it's my brain shutting down, knowing the temperature no longer matters. I keep sinking. I descend past the point where I think I'll hit the seabed. There is just more water. The water is infinite, like space. And I am space dust, reuniting with the cosmos.

I don't have to worry anymore. I no longer have to hold onto anything, or grasp for anything. I'm loosening my grip, and it's an immense relief. Happiness, freedom, peace. Just letting go of everything. If only I had known how to do this in life. It's a cruel trick to only learn this now, when it's too late.

I think of the beautiful life I've led. It wasn't all sunshine and roses—no one's life is—but it was a good life. I was a good daughter and sister. A good citizen, and a responsible guardian of the earth. Micro-memories flit into my mind: the time I lost a milk tooth in a playground swing accident, and had to suck on a block of ice and spit into the white porcelain sink till it stopped bleeding. I was spoilt rotten by the tooth fairy that night. A crisp five-pound note when I was used to getting a coin.

The time Jamie and I found huge inflatable bright pink flamingos in the pool at that cheap hotel at the coast and proceeded to spend the whole holiday floating in them and eating Eskimo Pies. I can smell the sunblock.

The time I met Becks: it was like a lightning strike of knowledge that she would be my person for the rest of my life. Like love at first sight, but deeper and without doubt.

My first boyfriend, first job, first flat. My first lover, my first orgasm, my first punch in the stomach that left me so winded I thought I was dying. My first climate change protest, when I finally felt part of a tribe. I could have done more; should have done more, but there's no time now for regrets.

I am feeling the cold, now. And I can feel the darkness pushing up against me, squeezing me. It's no longer a friendly embrace. It's black and sharp; an ebony razor, ready to slice. Frozen needles prick my soles and palms. The sense of peace dissolves into sudden panic as my lungs spasm, demanding oxygen—but the air is so far above me I think I'll never be able to reach it.

I love you, Alistair. I love you in a deep and primal way I've never loved anyone. You were so good me and my family. You woke me up to life's promises.

Becks, our souls will meet again—and then over and over until the end of time.

Jamie: I couldn't have asked for a better brother. Your huge heart is an inspiration.

Mom and Dad, thank you for everything. Your wise words, guidance, homegrown food, and steadfast values. Your tooth fairy money.

This is it. It's over. I send my final bid to the universe: may my loved ones be happy.

I let out a sob, and with it, my final pocket of air.

"What about Alexander?" booms Becks.

I have cold black mist in my head, I can't think clearly. I'm at the bottom of the ocean, so why can I hear my best friend's voice?

When she repeats herself, loud and clear, I realize she's waiting for a reply from me.

Yes, I reply. *And all my love to baby Alex, of course.* That sweet boy who I already love.

"That's not going to help him much, is it?" she demands. "Miserable missives from the deep."

Forever pragmatic.

No, I agree. *It won't help, but it's all I've got.*

"That's absolute bullshit, and you know it," she says.

I can't.

"You can't what?"

I can't anything. I'm dead.

The Becks I'm hallucinating roars with laughter. "That'll make an epic epitaph for your tombstone. I CAN'T. I'M DEAD." She continues to guffaw.

I'm glad you find my demise so entertaining.

"Oh, but darling, this is not the end for you."

It is, I reply. *I can feel it.*

"You can't feel shit. You're numb from the shock and the cold. That's not death. It's just an invitation. One you will not accept today."

You don't know how it feels.

"Fuck how it *feels.* FUCK HOW IT FEELS! Start kicking."

I can't feel my legs.

"Doesn't matter. Kick."

I try to kick, but my legs are useless. My lungs spasm with a final warning. I try again, and I feel my body move up slightly. I'm surprised, but in a relaxed way, as if it doesn't matter. As if I am separate to my body, indifferent, watching it go through the motions.

"Kick, goddammit," insists Becks. "Now. Before the weakness and confusion sets in."

Oxygen deprivation.

"Yes. You have to swim to the surface right now or it will be too late. Do you understand?"

I think I nod, but I can't be sure. I feel so weak. I will kick. I will swim to the surface. I just need a quick rest to gather my strength.

"NOW, Ivy."

Okay. Okay. I start moving my legs again without much progress.

"Think of Alistair," Becks says.

Alistair seems like a figment of my imagination.

"He'll never get over losing you."

Then I remember the gunshots, and seeing his body collapse.

Alistair's dead.

"He's not, Ivy. He's alive. He's one hundred percent alive."

Don't believe you.

"He's alive. And you know who else is alive? Jamie. Your folks. Baby Alex. And ME. And I'm not going to fucking lose you to some fucking psycho Russian bitch. Do you understand?"

Yes.

I kick. Not good. I try again. That's better.

"That's better," echoes Becks. "That's it. Keep going."

It's so far away.

"It's not. It just feels that way."

I kick.

"Think of Alistair, Ivy. And think of that little baby who needs you guys."

I kick harder. It's working. The darkness releases me from its hold. The water feels lighter around me, more like the ocean and less like a death grip. It gets easier to kick.

"You're almost there."

Am I? It feels miles away.

"Quickly, Ives. Quick as you can. Go, go, go."

Even though my head threatens to explode as I get closer to the surface, I keep going.

I see Alistair's sexy smile, eyes twinkling. I see baby Alex reaching for me, face alight with love.

I kick harder. My muscles cramp and my thoughts stutter. I'm not going to make it.

"You bloody well are," insists Becks.

I try use my arms now, too, pushing the dark depths away.

Alistair. Becks. Alex. Jamie.

I can get there. I can survive this.

"You already have," says Becks.

I break through the surface, splutter, then gasp in the biggest breath I've ever taken in my life.

CHAPTER 4
A Dark Kind of Luck

ALISTAIR

I wake up sweating after a fever dream that Ivy is in danger. She's just out of my reach and it's killing me that I can't help her. I'd rather die than stand by while she's in trouble. I need to get to her. I'm panting. It's so hot. Dark, humid, close. I blink but the room remains shrouded in darkness. I sit up; my torso is on fire. I feel the rough cotton of the bandages pulled tightly around my chest. I need to get out of here.

My mouth is stuck together. I'm so thirsty. Water.

I stand, even though it hurts like a motherfucker. Those bullets tore through skin, fracturing bone, without piercing any vital organs. Lucky—if you can call being shot twice in the chest by a Russian savage lucky. A dark kind of luck.

Standing is painful, but doable. A couple of cracked ribs is not the worst injury one can sustain. I try walking, my hands out in front of me to stop myself from clattering into furniture or walking into a wall. I'm panting again, my heart is pounding. Skin slicked with sweat. Agony does that.

While I can move, I know I won't get very far in this kind of pain. Pressing past the pain is one thing, but the body has limits the mind does not. Passing out is not an option. Not in a foreign country where you have Slavic assassins out to get you.

Anya's words come back to me. *Shortsighted. Revenge. Dividends.* She wants me alive, which is encouraging. She knows she'll make a great deal more money off my family if I'm still breathing. It makes my situation slightly less risky, and the gamble at escape less lethal.

I stumble around in the dark, trying to orient myself. There's not much to learn. The room is tiny, with bare brick walls, rough to the touch. A seemingly arbitrary black pole, like a curtain rod, is screwed into the wall, spanning the corner. The metal cot I've been sleeping on is the only furniture in the room. A small square window, acting as an air vent, is sealed with a dusty sharp-edged piece of metallic mesh. Perhaps I could tear it off. It would cost me a couple of days, lacerated palms, and probably some fingernails, but I might be able to do it. The frame isn't big enough for me to squeeze through, but maybe I can flag someone down depending on where the exterior is. I know it's not dead space on the other side because there is some airflow, some shadows, and subtle smells. Of course, it could be the room my jailer sits in, waiting for a hand to crush with his boot.

But that doesn't bear thinking about, because that small square is my only option. I'll take a couple of broken knuckles rather than no hope. I refuse to be a rat in a cage.

I sigh and immediately regret it as my ribs spark and flame.

I push the metal bed to the wall and climb onto it so the mesh is within easy reach. My eyes are habituated to the dark now—or at least as habituated as they can be in the pitch black. I run my fingers over the mesh. It's a shoddy job, but the loose screws are rusted in place, so I'm less optimistic that I'll be able to remove them. What I wouldn't do for Grayson's toolbox right now.

I start working on the corner, not caring that I can't see what I'm doing. Trusting my hands. I work at it for what feels like hours with little progress. Every time I want to give up, I think of Ivy, and that gives me the strength to push through the pain and boredom. Ivy is worth a hundred of these days; a thousand. My ribs are singing and my fingertips bleed, but I don't care.

There's a sound at the door. I move quickly to push the cot back to its original position, wiping the blood on the lone loose sheet and sitting on it. I'm sweating. It's the tropical humidity, but also the pain. I hear the key scraping in the lock, metal meeting metal, and then it turns, and the door opens. A muscular silhouette dominates the doorway with that hunched-over posture that over-trained weightlifters stalk around with. I shield my eyes. A naked bulb swings from the ceiling behind him. The light is dim, but it still hurts.

Arkadi grunts. I'm not sure if it's a greeting or a warning.

I will my fingertips to stop bleeding.

He has something in his hand, something I don't like the look of. An evil glint. A scalpel?

I try to talk but nothing comes out. Fear, thirst, lack of use. I swallow and try again. "What do you want?"

Arkadi grunts again. I can't see his face, only the outline of his bulk.

"You know my family," I say, voice gruff. "You know how much money we have. I can give you whatever you want."

"I already have what I want."

"I can give you more."

The man hawks and spits on the concrete floor. "You westerners. You think everything is for sale."

I feel a drop of blood fall from my hand. I smudge it with my foot. I'm glad it's dark.

"You Slavs," I reply. "You pretend you're not for sale."

Arkadi advances, and his bulk towers over me. It's not often I feel small, but the man's forearms are the size of my thighs. It's not a scalpel but a loaded syringe in his hand.

"What is that?" I ask.

I'm not afraid of needles, but I don't want whatever that junk is swimming in my veins.

Arkadi smirks. "It's a special cocktail, just for you. You like cocktails, *nyet?* Think of it as happy hour."

"Tell me what's in it," I say.

They wouldn't poison me—Anya wants me alive. Truth serum? I don't have any secrets they'd be interested in. They already know my ultimate weakness.

"Just relax," says Arkadi, taking a step closer. *"Prosto rass-lab'sya.* I have a bottle of water for you if you don't make trouble."

I take a breath, sending a spear of agony through my ribcage. I'm starving and dehydrated. I stand no chance fighting this orc of a man, so I offer him my shoulder and hope I'm not making a huge mistake.

The Russian jabs me and empties the syringe. God, I hate not knowing what it is. He smacks my shoulder afterward. *"Udachi.* For good luck," he smirks.

That's when the room starts spinning. I'm pressed down into the mattress by invisible hands, and my eyelids droop. The hazy silhouette leaves, but I'm out by the time he locks the door.

CHAPTER 5
Delirious with Death

IVY

I'm gasping, spluttering, hauling in air as if it's the last breath I'll ever take. My lungs, furious at being denied, spasm a few more times before finally relaxing into their regular rhythm. I'm still kicking, still crying, as the yacht's lights twinkle out of view. I spin to face the shore. It seems miles away. After that emotional tussle with the Grim Reaper down below, after kicking for my life, and I'm still going to drown.

I wait for Becks to argue, but she doesn't.

"Becks?" I whimper. "I need you."

But it seems that whatever guidance I got from her was only because I was delirious with death. The reality hits hard: I'm all alone in the middle of the fucking ocean. In a foreign country.

There's only one thing to do, which I'm sure Becks would agree with, and that is to start swimming to shore. If nothing else, it'll be better than treading water here and getting nowhere.

FML.

Honestly.

And with that, I start swimming. I go slowly but steadily, not stopping to rest, not wanting to waste time or energy on treading. I alternate between breast-stroke and freestyle. I can't remember which is the most efficient; breast-stroke feels easier, crawl feels faster.

I push through the acute urge to rest. I push away thoughts of how far away the glimmering beachfront is, because if I knew, I'd probably give up. I use my yoga training to turn the slow swimming into a kind of meditation, trying to ignore the darkness and fear. One stroke, then the next, then the next. It's all I have to do. Minutes turn into hours that feel like days. My biceps and forearms burn and my calves cramp. If I can get through this, I tell myself, I can get through anything.

I draw on the strength of the beautiful humans I know— Jamie pulling through his last bout of double pneumonia and the coma that followed, the Ravenscrofts getting through losing a daughter, and Ariana living through abduction and Stockholm Syndrome. They all survived, and so can I.

I kick harder, pull harder, and propel my body through the dark salty water. I can't help drawing the parallel between it and amniotic fluid. If I make it, maybe it'll feel like I've been reborn. It's one of many weird thoughts entering my head, but the idea of amniotic fluid keeps returning. It's the exhaustion talking. Or maybe it's my mum's energy reaching through space and time to hold me. I know that sometimes people who go into sensory deprivation tanks hallucinate. I seem to be emotionally hallucinating all over the place. As per my meditation training, I don't hold onto the strange thoughts, I just let them go and watch them unravel. One stroke, then the next, then the next.

I've been swimming for hours, I think; it's impossible to tell. My motivation to get to the shore is still strong, but my muscles are failing. I have used every ounce of energy. Still, I push myself to keep going, but I'm hardly moving. My limbs are no longer obeying my commands. I can see the land twinkling with lights, making me want to weep. So close, but out of reach. I can't give up, but I can't continue. I'm too tired to cry.

My last ditch effort at survival is to call for help. I doubt anyone will hear me, but sound does travel over water and I'm out of options. My first attempt is pathetic; my lungs are flat balloons. By the third attempt, I've achieved some volume.

"Help!" I shout. "HELP!"

I wish I knew the Thai word.

I follow my pleas with the shrillest scream I can muster, thinking the high-pitched sound might travel further.

It's so dark, and I'm getting so cold my teeth start chattering again. The exercise of swimming had been keeping my muscles warm, but now everything is fading. The warmth, my hope, my chance of surviving this shit-show.

My last scrap of energy goes into my last scream for help, and then I'm finished.

So close to shore. So cold and alone. Even Phantom Becks has deserted me.

I breathe in a mouthful of water by accident. I didn't realize I'd been sinking. I choke on it, retching, the salt stinging my eyes. Before I can clear my lungs completely, I aspirate another gulp. I panic, thrashing the water around me with energy I don't have, and then feel the water wash over my head.

CHAPTER 6
It Belongs To You

ALISTAIR

I wake up hours later from a dreamless sleep. No nightmares about Ivy, no panicky feeling that she's just out of my grasp. I don't know what that means. My eyelids are still heavy, but I can open them enough to see the bottle of water on the floor. I lunge for it, snatch it up and down it, leaving only one sip for later.

There is muted light coming from the window, casting everything in gray. I'm guessing the jab was a potent painkiller, and probably—hopefully—an antibiotic. They wouldn't want me dying of an infection after all they've done to keep me alive so far. Hopefully, food will be part of the survival strategy, because I am shaking with hunger. I can't yet muster up the energy to continue work on peeling back that mesh.

Instead, I push the bed back against the wall and lean my back up against the cold concrete. I welcome the coolness of it. This country is so fucking hot. Thank god for cool walls and antibiotics.

That last sip of water is calling to me, but I must wait. I don't know when the next bottle is coming, and what conditions it will entail. I lean my head back and count my breaths, forcing myself to slow them down. I try to avoid thinking of Ivy, because she is my kryptonite. I feel very little fear until she pops into my mind—then suddenly my pulse is racing. It's absolute torture not knowing where or how she is. I remember her in the dark ocean, the black waves pulling her under. The bullets exploding the water around her. My jaw is so tightly clenched that my teeth are in danger of cracking.

I breathe through the fear. The guilt, the grief. The chances of her being alive are close to zero, I know, but the only thing that will get me through this is thinking that she survived, so that is what I will do. It may be an imaginary path, but at least it's a path. I pray—to a god I don't believe in—to keep her safe until I find her. I picture her alive and well. Wearing that sundress, sweeping her hair out of her face, and laughing. Yes. She's fine.

I let myself rest in that hope. My jaw relaxes.

Surviving this will require prime mental strength that can't afford useless and defeating emotions like worry and guilt.

The love of my life is okay. My only job here is to stay alive and find my way back to her.

I close my eyes and see her, the light fabric of her dress rippling in the breeze. We're at the house in Koh Samui, out on the bright patio. The image of the sparkling blue pool adds to my thirst, so I pick up a spiced rum cocktail and we chink glasses. The drink is gloriously cold as it fills my mouth and flows down my throat. I lick my lips at the pleasure of it. I'm tanned and strong as I pull Ivy into a hug and kiss her head. Her hair is fragranced with the shampoo of mine that she likes—cedar and spice. I hold her and breathe her in as if I can absorb her completely. Ivy luxuriates in my embrace, then pushes me away, giggling, when she feels my erection through my board shorts. She steps backward, mischievous eyes glinting, index finger waving.

"Oh, no, not yet," she teases, her ever-generous smile showing off white teeth. "You're going to have to wait."

"I don't want to wait," I reply. "I want to fuck you right now."

"So impatient," Ivy admonishes. "That won't get you anywhere."

I grab her wrist. "I need you," I say. "I need you more than I've ever needed you."

"Well," she says. "You're going to have to watch me, first."

My cock twitches. "Watch you?"

Ivy giggles and nods, then presses me back into a sun lounger. "Drink up," she says. "You'll need your energy after this."

I settle into the seat and look at Ivy, marveling at how I get to spend time with such an entrancing creature. "You're so fucking beautiful."

She waves off the compliment, slugs her cocktail, and clicks play on her phone. It's a song I don't recognize, but it certainly belongs on a bedroom playlist.

Her brows arch. "You ready?"

"Yes, ma'am," I reply.

Ivy starts moving her body to the music, slowly at first, shyly. Then she starts getting more into it and her hips move in a way that makes me want to pin her down and ravage her. I adjust my seat without breaking eye contact.

Ivy's feeling the beat. Her face relaxes, her movements get more fluid. She's enjoying this, but not as much as I am. She undoes the first button and winks at me. I clear my throat and straighten my spine. The next button, and the next, until I see the swell of her tits. She gazes at me as she strokes herself, moving to the bass-heavy tune. All my blood has rushed to my cock. I don't stand a chance.

Fourth, fifth, sixth button, and she drops the flimsy dress to the ground. It lands with a shimmer. She is more tanned than I ever remember seeing her, and her white bikini sets it off perfectly. She lifts her arms to the music and turns in a circle, showing off every angle of her perfect body.

"You're perfect," I say. "And I'm not just referring to your body."

She bites her bottom lip and smiles. "You're referring to my intellect, then?"

I nod. "Your intellect, your warmth, your curiosity, your sense of humor. I'm in love with it all."

Ivy dances closer, just out of my reach, and slowly pulls the bow that releases her bikini top. It also lands on the warm tiles below.

"And what about my pussy?" she asks. "Do you love my pussy?"

I can't stand waiting anymore. I grab her wrist and pull her down to me with a growl. "Your pussy is the thing I love most of all."

Ivy giggles. "Most of all?"

"Most of all," I confirm. "It's the most incredible pussy I've ever encountered."

"More incredible, than, say, my sparkling personality?"

I pretend to consider the question. "That would be a close call, but yes."

"You're terrible." Ivy laughs but doesn't resist me pulling her bright bikini bottoms off.

She squeals in surprise as I quickly spin her onto the lounger. I kneel between her legs.

"This pussy," I say, shaking my head. "This pussy is everything."

"Stop," says Ivy, "you're making her shy."

"This pussy isn't shy. It's a powerhouse."

Ivy guffaws. "A *powerhouse?*"

I nod. "A powerhouse of pleasure. And it's all fucking mine."

I lower my head and kiss the inside of her thigh, caressing the creamy skin with my lips and tongue. As I get nearer to the *powerhouse*, I suck harder, making Ivy moan. I grit my teeth, feeling primal.

"This pussy will always be mine," I growl, as I latch onto it with my hungry mouth.

Ivy gasps, but she doesn't move away.

"Fuck," she says, her breath coming in little gasps. "Yes. It belongs to you."

I suck and swirl and plunge my tongue into her until I can feel her muscles quivering, then I go harder and faster. Her moans tell me she's right on the edge.

"Come for me," I drawl, letting my words vibrate on her clit. I thrust my tongue inside one more time and Ivy yells, her muscles contracting as she writhes in pleasure.

"Fuck, Alistair, fuck!" she moans, pulsating on my tongue. I bite her inner thigh just hard enough to leave a mark, then gather her up into my arms till she stops shaking.

CHAPTER 7
Bollocks

IVY

The next moments are dark, blurry and confused. A man's voice shouting rapid-fire words that I don't understand. A slap through my face that doesn't sting because I'm frozen numb. Chaotic chatting and yelling while I cough out what feels like a gallon of salt water, my body shaking so hard I think I'm having a seizure. Blankets cover me; palms whack my back—like a doctor smacking a newborn baby. I have indeed been reborn.

I am hoisted and carried, still dripping, into a tuk-tuk. A miniature disco ball hangs from the ceiling of the vehicle and I am entranced by it. In my mixed-up thoughts, I think I may have died, and the disco ball is the sign that I'm in a weird vibrating heaven. An ambulance disco. My saviors keep talking to me in rushed Thai. Thoughts come, short and muddled:

They smell like fish.

There was a boat.

Did they hear me scream?

They are fishermen.

They are also dripping wet.

They saved my life.

I need their names.

Alistair will reward them.

If Alistair is alive.

I must pass out in the tuk-tuk because the next thing I remember is the fishermen yelling at the reception staff in a clean white hospital emergency room. Are we still on the island? We must be. I didn't know there was a hospital in Koh Samui, but here we are. I falter and almost fall, but the men yank my cooked-noodle body up to stop me from face-planting. We're dripping water on the pristine floor tiles, but no one seems to care. A gurney arrives, and I am helped onto it and pressed down. The fishermen pat me as if to say *You'll be okay now.*

"Thank you." It comes out like a sob. "*Kob kun khrap. Kob kun khrap.*"

They wave away my thanks as if it's all in a day's work. I wonder how often they need to haul their boat out in the middle of the night to save hapless tourists.

"Name?" I ask. "Names?" but they don't understand. Before I can ask again, the walls are moving and the overhead lights are flashing. The nurses are rolling me away.

There's a new flurry of activity with medical staff slapping stickers on me and covering my face with an oxygen mask. The clean, cool air hisses into my nose and mouth. My wet clothes are cut off, and an electric blanket is placed over me, followed by a crinkly silver space blanket. IV. Fluids. Blood pressure cuff. They check my irises' reaction to their penlight and frown at what they observe. I feel the beginning of warmth blooming on my torso. I relax into it and pass out again.

When I come to, the manic bustling is over, and I'm in a quiet room with just one nurse watching over me. When he sees me open my eyes, he nods and makes a call. What feels like just seconds later, and man bursts through the door. For a moment I think it must be Alistair, and my heart soars.

"Ivy!" Henderson exclaims.

Not Alistair.

A split second of crushing disappointment is followed by intense relief and gratitude to see a familiar face.

"Henderson," I croak, and the tears spill down my cheeks. "Is Alistair ... alive?" The question alone makes me shudder with grief.

"Hey," he says, expressing concern. He takes my hand and sits on the edge of the bed. I've never seen him so quietly gentle. "Hey, hey, hey. Don't cry."

The fact that he doesn't immediately answer "Yes" makes me cry harder.

"Tell me," I beg. I need to know.

His voice is soft. "We don't know."

My tears stream. How can this be happening?

"Don't cry," he says, squeezing my hand. "He'll be fine."

"You don't know that."

"He will be. Alistair is a survivor. He's tougher than anyone I know."

"You didn't see what I saw," I cry.

Henderson's forehead creases. "You need to tell me what happened."

"She shot him," I cry. "Well, her thug did. Twice."

His face pales. "He could have missed."

I shake my head, tears dripping from the tip of my nose. "He fell. It wasn't an act."

"A bullet-proof vest, then," says Henderson.

"On a party yacht?" I say, voice breaking. I'm shaking with emotion. "No."

He's just as frantic to believe Alistair is alive. I get a sticky panicky feeling. I was desperate to think that he would know exactly what to do in this situation, but he sits there with pain in his eyes, looking just as lost as I feel.

"People survive gunshot wounds all the time," he assures me—or maybe he's trying to convince himself.

"Yes," I agree. Maybe not *all the time*, but I concede the point. "As you say, he's a survivor."

"And we haven't found ... we haven't found his ... *body*. So that's a good sign."

His body.

I want to scream. How can this be happening? I cover my face with my hands, hoping it will all just go away. Henderson rubs the back of his neck, then looks into my eyes. "I won't give up hope if you won't."

Ugh, poor Henderson. I think of him as a small child in a hospital like this, hearing that his father and best friend had been killed. How can anyone heal from that? I cry harder. For little Henderson— for a lifetime without his father's love—and for Alistair, the love of my life. He can't be dead. I won't believe it.

"We need to find him," I say.

Henderson's expression changes, and his sharp focus returns. "We're on it. The team is searching. No sign of him on the yacht or in the ocean—no blood, either. No one matching his description in any of the hospitals."

"There's more than one on the island?"

Henderson's lips quirk into an almost-smile. It's a welcome

sight. "Yes. I happen to have visited every one of them looking for you two."

"Thank you," I say. "Thank you for always looking after us."

His expression darkens again. "I should have been on that yacht. The host didn't allow bodyguards."

"Yeah, that would have been ... awkward."

His eyes burn into mine. "I don't give a fuck. My only job is to protect Alistair, and now he's missing."

"Through no fault of yours," I say.

His jaw muscles ripple as he clenches his teeth, working through his anger. "If only that were true."

"What do we do now?" I ask Henderson, sweeping my blankets off, ready to stand.

"Oh, no, no, no." He shakes his head. "You're not doing anything. You're supposed to be resting."

"*Resting?*" I demand, mouth open like a guppy. "Are you fucking kidding me?"

"Er..." Henderson's eyes narrow. "Ivy, I don't think you know how close you came to dying back there."

"I do," I reply. I honestly thought it was the end. "I heard voices and everything. But now I'm fine. I'm coming with you."

"I doubt your doctor would allow that."

I fling my legs over the side of the bed. "Alistair is the one we should be worried about. I'm okay."

"Uh…" he motions at the hospital equipment beeping beside my bed. "You're attached to all kinds of things there. They look kind of important."

"Bollocks," I reply. "I'm fine."

I stand up—or, rather, try to stand up—and my knees buckle instantly, pulling my IV stand down with me. Henderson launches himself forward, catching me just before I face-plant, and grabs the stand before it hits me.

Ever gracious, he doesn't say, "I told you so," but rather helps me back into the hospital bed and covers me with the blankets again.

I thank him sheepishly, blinking back tears of frustration.

"I get it," he murmurs. "You want to help. But I promise you we're doing absolutely everything we can to find him. Alistair would want you to recover properly, right?"

I swipe at my tears, swallow the lump in my throat, and nod.

"You need to focus on regaining your strength so that when we need you, you'll be ready to help. Okay?"

I nod again. I'm still dying to leave the hospital to search for Alistair, but I know I'm not thinking straight. I know Henderson is right.

"Where do you think he is?" I whisper.

Henderson sighs. "I think they have him."

CHAPTER 8

Dirty Floor

ALISTAIR

I wake up with a throbbing cock. My dreams of Ivy are so realistic I can almost smell her. God, I can almost taste her. She takes me out of this bleak prison to a place filled with light and pleasure. I sigh deeply, wondering if I'll ever get to kiss her again. I have given up on tearing the mesh from the wall. It was blind optimism thinking I'd ever be able to shift it without a tool. My fingertips are fucked from trying, and it hardly made a difference. I'll use the energy Ivy gives me for a more productive cause, something that will actually help me get out of here.

The basement is twelve by eight. Concrete walls mottled with humidity stains—dark patches spreading like the rash of a tropical disease. The constant darkness softens the harsh edges of my cell.

Ivy. Her memory cuts through the gloom sharper than any light. The way she'd tuck her hair behind her ear, that small laugh that always means something more. Not just a memory—a lifeline.

I roll onto the dirty floor.

Twelve push-ups. Twelve squats. Each movement deliberate. I use the black pole to do pull-ups. Ten, twenty, thirty. My body is remembering how to be strong, how to survive.

The Russians think they've broken me. They don't understand. Every moment here is another moment closer to getting back to her. This space is just another problem to solve, another obstacle between me and Ivy.

Ambient sounds filter through: distant motorcycle engines, muffled voices in Thai. The squealing of rats that makes my spine itch. The floor feels solid beneath me—pocked concrete scattered with dust bunnies and paint chips. Every time I feel like giving up, I picture Ivy's face. I picture baby Alex. I move on to pull-ups. The next time the Russian fucks come in here, I'll be ready.

CHAPTER 9
Don't You Dare Fucking Die

IVY

It's thirty-two hours later when I wake up. I don't know if it was pure exhaustion that knocked me out, or if Henderson asked the doctor to slip a little sedative into my IV line to prevent me from escaping. My eyes feel glued together; my throat is absolutely desiccated. I prize open one eye to search for water, reach for it, and gulp it down. The relief is instant. I swish the water around in my mouth. It's cool and delicious. When I finally sit up, the room is unrecognizable. Every single nook and cranny is bursting with flowers, tropical fruit, bottles of champagne, and chocolate boxes. My heart leaps. Alistair? Only Alistair would be responsible for such a lavish display. My heart accelerates—I feel like it's beating right at the top of my chest, fast and furious. Could it be?

I blink fast, trying to clear the haziness in my vision. There'll be a card, surely. I'll find a card with Alistair's name on it. This time, I get out of bed as slowly as I can, excitement notwithstanding. My knees threaten to collapse again, but I urge them to keep me up for just long enough to hunt for the card. I wheel my IV stand along with me toward a giant pot of orchids and snatch the card from the base, searching for only one word. It isn't there.

Dear Ivy

We were so sorry to hear about the incident.

We're on our way and will be with you soon.

Please be assured that we will do whatever it takes to find Alistair.

In the meantime, you must focus solely on your recovery.

You are a valued member of our family, and Alistair and baby Alex will need you in your best health.

Sincerely, The Ravenscrofts

The handwritten words swim, and don't make much sense. The word I'm looking for does not appear in the correct place, and my spirits plummet. I search for another card, suspecting I already have my answer, but refusing to accept it. I go to the champagne. That's more Alistair's style.

St Ives, WTAF.

On my way.

Don't you dare fucking die.

Love you

Becks

I snort out a mirthless laugh. *Don't you dare fucking die.* Little does Becks know that she's the one who dragged me up from the saltwater abyss. It'll make a good story one day, when we're sharing this bottle, but for now, it's a punch in the gut, confirming that Alistair is still missing.

There are also flowers from my family, including a hospital-gift-store Pokémon character from Jamie that makes me think of the giant squirrel Alistair bought him, and my eyes flood. I take the toy to bed and sob into its soft yellow fabric. It looks like I'll soon be surrounded by people, but right now, I'm the saddest and loneliest I've ever been. I shake my head, letting the sobbing take over my whole body.

How did we get here? How did things turn so terrible, so fast? My heart aches so much it threatens to choke me as I completely give in to the despair.

CHAPTER 10

Mantra

ALISTAIR

I've lost track of time. Days blur into a continuous dark membrane. I'm not sure if I've been here for hours or days. It's always dark, apart from the minuscule amount of light the screen lets through. Concrete everywhere. Always concrete. Tiny fractures like dried riverbeds spread across its surface.

The room smells of stale sweat and mildew, with an underlying chemical tang—something industrial. Bleach. Diesel. My own body odor layered over everything, rank and sour. The air feels thick, almost viscous, pressing against my skin with tropical humidity. Condensation beads on the walls, tracing slow paths.

My food arrives through a small hatch—barely wide enough to push a metal tray through. Rice. Some unidentifiable protein. Bland. Calculated. At first I rejected it, but now that I'm training, I need the fuel. The metal tray is scratched, dented. Someone else's history embedded in its surface.

My captors won't tell me what they want from me or if they have contacted my family yet. I'm assuming the ransom will be on the hefty side. If it's solely revenge they're after, I wouldn't be alive, so my bet is on a generous ransom package. I just hope that Christopher doesn't do anything stupid. Mother will rein him in. I hope.

And Ivy? Ivy who I pushed into the sea. She'll be furious with me. She'd better be. I can take it. A furious Ivy is a breathing Ivy.

She's alive, I keep telling myself. *She's alive. She's alive.*

It's the mantra that keeps me sane.

Or sane enough, anyway, to plan my escape.

CHAPTER 11
Noah

IVY

The door opens gently, and I look up, desperate to see a familiar face. When I see it's my best friend, I crumple.

"Oh!" Becks exclaims when she sees me. "Oh, poor, poor Ivy." Her mouth is open, as are her arms as she envelopes me. "Oh, my poor friend. What have they done to you?"

She sits on my bed while she hugs me, letting me cry on her shoulder. "I'm okay," I murmur, my shuddering breath telling a different story. "I'm okay. Just worried sick about Alistair."

"Of course you are."

"What if he's dead, Becks? What if they killed him?"

"This is Alistair we're talking about," she says. "No one kills Alistair. He's, like, the main character in an action movie.

The one that never dies. The one they want you to think has died, but then he shows up with just a few scratches."

"Invincible," I say.

She smacks my arm. "Exactly! Sorry, was that too hard? Are you hurt?"

I shake my head. "Not hurt. But I did see my life flash before my eyes while I was drowning."

"I better have been in your highlight reel," says Becks.

"Of course you were. You *were* my highlight reel. Also, I had this surreal come-to-god moment when I'd given up, and you were kicking my ass to swim to shore."

"So ... basically, I saved your life."

"Basically, yes."

"You owe me a fancy dinner, then."

"We can drink the champagne," I say.

I want to banter with her, but I feel dark inside; like there's a black hole that sucks any positive emotion.

"When are you getting out of here?"

I shrug. "I've been sleeping. Haven't spoken to a doctor yet."

"Say no more," Becks announces. "I will gather your release information and take you somewhere nice to drink champagne." She clears her throat. "I mean, to *recover*."

"The two are not mutually exclusive," I reply.

"That's my girl," Becks says, squeezing my knee. "Wish me luck when I speak to the doctors. The only Thai I know, I learned from that seedy massage place in Brighton."

"Best to speak English, then?" I suggest.

"Nonsense! Where's the fun in that?" She winks at me and moves to leave the room. That's when I notice the man standing at the door as if he's been there all along.

"Oh!" Becks exclaims, spinning back to face me, a school-girl grin on her face. "This is Noah."

I blink, confused. "Noah?"

I search my memory for anything about a Noah, and come up blank.

"Don't be mad. I've been keeping him a secret. I didn't want to steal your billionaire thunder. We've been together for a month now."

"A *month?*" I repeat. This is highly unusual. First, that she would keep a lover from me. Second, that she's been with him for a month. No one gets to stay in Becks's bed that long. Thirdly, what's he doing in Thailand?

Another reason I'm confused is because I see the way she looks at Henderson, and it's not a platonic gaze.

"Okay," I say. "Congratulations?"

"I'll spill all the tea when I get back," she winks. "In the meantime, I'm off to ask about your happy ending."

"Well," I sigh after Becks leaves the room. "This isn't awkward at all."

Noah chuckles and approaches to shake my hand. "Pleased to finally meet you. As you can imagine, Becks has told me so much about you."

"Again, not awkward at all," I reply, this time with a smile. "You've really been together for that long?"

"Yep," he nods, sliding his hands in his pockets. "And I'm not gonna let her go. Becks is amazing."

"We already have something in common, then," I say.

I feel a distinct sense of unease. I don't want to focus on anything but finding Alistair, but I'm in a flower-filled room with a stranger who's smiling as if it's an ordinary day; an ordinary introduction.

"Are you okay?" Noah asks.

Had I been scowling at him? Don't know, don't care. I need to get out of here.

"No," I reply. "I'm not okay. I need to get out of here."

"I'm sure Becks will make that happen," he assures me. "She has a knack for getting things done."

I carefully remove the IV. It's a relief to be free of it. I look down at my flimsy hospital gown and vaguely remember the emergency staff cutting my wet clothes off.

"Oh," says Noah, "we brought this." He holds up a neat little backpack.

I blink, waiting for him to explain.

"Clothes," he blurts. "Old jeans and a T-shirt. Flip-flops. And a toothbrush. Bamboo. Becks insisted."

I thank him and take the backpack into the bathroom to change. My knee function has returned, thank god, instead of being hinges made of jelly.

"I can pack up while you change, if you like," Noah says, gesturing to the hills of flowers in the room. "Although... you may need to hire an actual truck to transport this jungle."

He's trying to be nice, trying to keep it light, but I can't bring myself to laugh. Not even the people-pleaser in me can force a hint of a smile. I close the bathroom door and pull on the torn jeans and shirt. When I open the door again, Becks is back.

"So-o-o-o," she sidles up to me. "While they didn't *actually* approve my request to break you out of here, they did say you probably wouldn't die if I took you somewhere you can rest, and have lots of fluids."

Their two faces search mine, waiting for an answer.

I nod. "Sounds good enough to me."

"Also," adds Becks, "it probably helps that your hospital bill has been paid in full, and then some."

I say a quick silent prayer to the Mother of Ravens. *Thank you, Isobel.*

"Talking about bills," I say. "Let me know what I owe you for coming all the way out here."

"Oh, don't worry about that," says Noah, "I was happy to pay. I've never been to Thailand before, and I had tons of air miles."

Becks grins. She has this weird soft look in her eyes that I'm not sure I like. I want to vet this man before she gets attached, but it looks like I'm too late.

CHAPTER 12
Dada

ALISTAIR

The smell of concrete and mold, the metallic undertone of stale sweat. My breath echoes in the confined space, a rhythmic sound that keeps time with my movement. My muscles ache, but that doesn't stop me. Every time I reach failure, I push through it for one more rep. Always one more rep. Ivy gets me through the pain, the hunger, the boredom. Her love is keeping me alive. I don't allow myself to worry about her; thinking of her hurt or in pain is soul-destroying. I throw up seven-inch-thick steel walls in my mind whenever an anxious thought approaches. Denial is my best friend in here. Denial gets me strong. Denial allows me to believe in an ultimate reality where Ivy is healthy and thriving—showing the world how damn incredible she is. And I'll be there by her side, supporting her, loving her, worshipping her in every way.

A memory materializes with painful clarity: Baby Alex, his cheeks flushed and round, grinning in pure, unbridled joy. Happy and bouncy, lifting his arms to me when I walk into the room. He learns his first few words.

"Dada," he says. "Up."

His voice is a promise. My heart expands.

Now Ivy is wearing that summer dress and twirling in the warm golden air, laughing and calling me over. Her laugh cuts through the basement's oppressive silence. I take Alex, and we embrace each other, swaying in the sunshine that exists only in my mind.

I sigh deeply. It will happen. I will make it happen.

I assume my position and wait. Muscles coiled. Mind sharp. Ready.

CHAPTER 13
Two Unlit Matches

IVY

On our way out, Noah snags the bottle of champagne and I grab the Pokémon from Jamie and push it into the backpack. I hand a couple of boxes of chocolate to Becks, scoring another wide grin from her. I hope the staff will enjoy the rest of the gifts and flowers.

The air outside the hospital is warm and humid, so different from the cool, disinfected air I'd been breathing inside. The sun is warm on my skin, and I feel it melt some of the tension in my body. A sense of calm settles over me.

It's going to be okay, I tell myself. *We'll find Alistair and everything will be okay.*

"I need to tell Henderson," I say to Becks. "He'll panic if he finds that hospital room empty."

She smiles. "Already done!"

"I'm guessing he's furious with me?"

"With *us,* yes. But I promised I'd take good care of you. Not let you go out till you're better."

"I *am* better," I reply. "My knees are holding me up, now. The last time Henderson saw me, I almost lost my front teeth."

"Not a good look," she replies. "I can see why he insisted you stay."

I sigh. "He'll hate me for this."

"He'll hate me more," replies Becks.

She's probably right. The two of them definitely have chemistry. When they're in a room together, they're like two unlit matches.

We hop into a taxi with faded paintwork. Noah tries to help me into the car, but I wave him off. I'm sure he's a lovely guy, but I find his presence unnecessary. I'm anxious and irritable, and I just want to know that Alistair is safe. My disdain doesn't go unnoticed, but Becks—rather graciously, I'll admit—keeps her feelings to herself as the driver puts his foot down.

The hotel is cheap and cheerful, and right on the beachfront. Perfect. The last thing I want right now is luxury. It wouldn't feel right. I'm itching to go out and look for Alistair, but I have no idea where to start. Becks won't let me out of her sight, so there's also that.

"Don't make me regret breaking you out of the hospital," she warns, wagging her chipped-nail-polish finger at me.

"Yes, ma'am," I reply, looking suitably scolded.

Noah orders room service—coconut curry and a fruit platter—and we take it out onto the little wooden deck. I tell them what happened on the yacht, and Becks pales at the twist.

"I'm sorry, did I hear you right? Moneybags pushed you over the side of a fucking sex yacht?"

"Probably saved your life," says Noah.

She glares at him. "She almost fucking *drowned*."

He shrugs. "Better than being shot by a Russian assassin."

We don't admit that he's right. After all, I made it back. Alistair did not.

"What's the plan?" asks Becks. "To find him?"

I sigh, pushing the food away. My throat's too tight to eat, anyway. "Henderson didn't give me any details. Just said that they'll find him."

I'd love to say that people don't disappear, but I know that's not true. Not when the mafia is involved.

"Well," sighs Becks. "If anyone can find him, Henderson will. That's a bromance like I've never seen before."

"Yes, well, they have a complicated past."

Noah nods. "Trauma bonding."

I wish he wouldn't talk. I know I'm being a bitch, but I can't help it. I wish Becks hadn't brought him, but then I remember he's the one who paid for the flights. It was super generous, and I need to check myself. If she really does have feelings for him, I need to at least get to know him before having any kind of opinion.

"You should eat," urges Becks. "You'll need your strength."

"You sound like my mother," I reply.

"Exactly. Your mum made me promise that I'd take care of you. Which reminds me…" she reaches for her handbag, a scuffed time-softened leather satchel that I love. "She gave me this."

I frown at the envelope. It's addressed to me. When I turn it over, I see that it's from my bank.

"Why would Mum send this with you?"

Becks purses her lips. "I don't know. She said it was important."

"She opened it?"

Becks is non-committal. "She *is* your mum."

"Cheeky," I say, pulling the letter out of the neatly torn envelope.

My eyes bulge when I read the statement. My heart beats in my ears. "Holy shit."

"Tell us!" insists Becks. "I know it's not bad news because your mom had this glint in her eye when she gave it to me."

"It's not bad news," I whisper.

"It's Alistair."

"What do you mean?"

I look at the date. "Last week. Alistair paid off my entire student debt."

"Holy shit," echoes Becks, eyes wide. "That's incredible. You're free!"

My sinuses sting, and my eyes fill with tears. I don't hold back the ugly cry.

On any other day I'd be whooping with joy. But I'm not free. I'm devastated. I've lost the first man who I truly and fiercely loved, and who loved me with the same fire and intensity.

Becks hold me while I sob, and my tears soak her shirt.

CHAPTER 14
Animal in a Cage

ALISTAIR

I hear him coming. When Arkadi opens the metal door, I'm ready.

I launch myself straight into the door, kicking it into him with all my power. The food tray clatters to the concrete floor, and the plastic plate breaks in half. The orc of a man is still standing, but he's doubled over, hands grasping his head where the metal slammed into his skull. Dark blood seeps through the gaps in his fingers as he tries to wipe it away, grunting. I get the feeling he's moaning in anger rather than pain—given his brick-shithouse physique, I don't think this bloke feels much pain at all.

Adrenaline is rushing through me. He won't be disoriented for long. I know it's now or never, but he's blocking my way. I step back, then roundhouse kick the door again. The heavy metal will do more damage than my bare foot. But my angle isn't right, and it sends a shooting pain up my leg without doing much more damage to Arkadi.

He notices me limp backward; a cornered animal in a cage.

I scramble for the broken plate. It's too flimsy. I pick up the stainless steel tray instead. When Arkadi throws a punch my way, I intercept it with my makeshift shield. The blow sends vibrations through my arms, which I welcome because it's a whole lot better than this guy's fist buried in my face. I kick him in the nuts and almost break my foot. He grunts and lunges for me, his meaty mitts almost catching me by the throat. My ankle is properly fucked now, which will complicate my escape.

Just think of Ivy, I tell myself.

I launch myself at the orc with renewed strength. Smashing my fist into his jaw. There is a sickening crunching sound as we connect. At least one of my fingers breaks, but it's worth it, because his jaw dislocates in slow motion—at least, that's what it feels like. He spits blood on the floor, then lifts his gaze to me. Fucking hell, he's a mountain of muscle. He doesn't take his eyes off me as he uses both hands to force his jaw back into place with a stomach-churning wet crack of cartilage and bone. The violence in his eyes, along with the awful sound, dissolves my stomach. I'm absolutely fucked, and we both know it.

Arkadi's going to fucking kill me. I can see it in the set of his jaw. He's going to rip me limb from limb.

"Wait," I say, trying to buy some time.

"*Nyet,*" he replies, launching himself at me.

I'm able to dodge his first lunge, which only makes him angrier. Arkadi yells in fury.

His temper may be my only way out of this. Perhaps the blood coursing through his rope-like veins to power his muscles will starve his brain of oxygen. I just need a moment of distraction to bolt past him.

Now or never.

Using explosive movement, I dart past his meaty torso, but the space is too narrow, and he is too fast. He grabs me by the throat, clotheslining me. I choke. Air completely cut off, throat crushed, I can do nothing but collapse. I'm in a dark vacuum of oxygen deprivation, trapped in a black hole, seeing stars. Fuck.

A sudden sharp pain in my stomach tells me I've been kicked. I curl up instinctively to protect myself, but the blows keep coming. There's a warm metallic taste in my mouth. I spit the blood out and get rewarded with a boot to the face, shattering my cheekbone.

No. His temper isn't going to help me escape. It's going to kill me.

I'm a tight ball on the hard concrete floor. When he can't reach my stomach with his kicks anymore, he directs them at my kidneys, making me cry out in agony.

A slow death, then. Pulverization. Blow by bitter blow.

I think of Mariya, and all the other lives I have destroyed.

It's what I deserve.

But Alex doesn't deserve this—to be orphaned again. Ivy doesn't deserve this. I need to get up, or I'll die on this floor, away from home, away from everyone I love.

Shallow breath rasping in my damaged throat, I try to stand. Arkadi immediately slams me down again. I hear something dislocate with a wet crunch, but can't tell where it came from. The pain signals are a crazed choir without a conductor. I try again, knowing it will end in anguish, but also that I can't give up. I drag my broken body upright, and this time Arkadi lets me. When I open my eyes, he's grinning at me, cruel eyes sparkling. It's much more entertaining to punch someone standing than to kick a sack of potatoes on the floor. He curls his mitt into a fist. I know this is going to be the strike that ends it; a neck-snapping punch to put me out of my misery, and there's nothing I can do to stop it.

Defeated, I close my eyes. An atheist's last prayer. I wait for the end, but hear an angel talking, instead. An angel with an accent straight out of Moscow.

"Arkadi," Anja scolds in a dangerous whisper. "You *know* that we need him alive."

CHAPTER 15
He's Not Dead

IVY

Noah excuses himself to go for a run. I don't blame him, I'm a complete mess.

"Excellent," says Becks after he leaves. She rubs her hands together. "Now we can spill."

I have nothing to spill. I'm empty of everything except heartache and worry. She fetches red wine and two stemless glasses.

"I'm sorry I haven't been very friendly to Noah," I say. "Everything is just too much at the moment."

"You don't have to worry about Noah," Becks says. "He's a grown-ass man with perspective. He's not expecting anything from you. We're here to support you."

"Thank you," I reply. "I can't believe you came all this way."

"Are you crazy?" she demands. "You were found half-drowned in a foreign country. The man that was supposed to be looking after you is missing. There is no reality in which I *wouldn't* have come."

"I keep forgetting that; about the drowning. All I can think about is Alistair. Do you think he's alive?"

"It doesn't matter what I think," shrugs Becks. "But, yes, I'd guess he's alive. Seeing as they haven't found proof otherwise."

Proof.

She means a dead body.

But I can't even imagine Alistair like that. Pale skin, lifeless eyes.

I shake my head.

He's not dead.

He's not dead.

He's not dead.

"Yes," I agree. "I'll believe he's alive unless proven otherwise."

"It's the only way to stay sane," says Becks.

I take a long sip of wine. "Yes."

We sit in companionable silence for a while, looking up at the stars; lost in our own thoughts.

"I want to go look for him," I admit.

Becks puts her glass down. "Of course you do. And if there was any chance of you finding him, I wouldn't blame you for trying."

I think of Henderson out there trying to find his lifetime friend. "Did you let Henderson know you broke me out of the hospital?"

Becks pulls a grimace. "Not exactly. I didn't want him to—"

"We have to tell him," I say.

"I told the hospital staff to let him know the next time he calls for an update on you. Thought it would give us some time before he explodes at me."

"Yeah, he's not going to be happy."

"Henderson can sulk all he likes. His job is to look after his friend, and my job is to look after you."

"Thank you."

Becks rubs my arm. "No one should have to go through what you've been through these last few weeks. It's ridiculous."

"I was just getting over the PTSD from the Jeff incident," I say. "Now this."

"Fucking hell. Good thing you can afford a therapist."

"That's a silver lining right there," I say, raising my glass to her.

I wish I could relax into this time together, wish I could be peaceful and calm for just a little while, but my body is on high alert: heart hammering, thoughts racing, stomach clenched. I won't be able to relax until they find Alistair.

Beck's phone pings. "Ah," she says. "The Ravenscrofts are in Thailand. Just landed."

"And you would know this how?"

"I have eyes everywhere," she jokes. Or at least, I think she's joking.

We're quiet for a little while, eyes searching the night sky for answers it cannot reveal.

"Is it worth it?" Becks asks.

"Is what worth it?"

"All the trauma. The danger. Is the sex really that good?"

I want to reply that it's not about the sex, but it's not a hundred percent true. The sex is a huge part of our compulsion for one another. How could it not be? It's incredible, mind-blowing, transformative. But deep down I know I'm not in love with the sex. I'm in love with Alistair.

"The short answer is yes," I reply.

Becks raises her eyebrows. "Wow."

"This relationship with Alistair has blown my life wide open. It's changed me on every level." I turn to face Becks. "I feel more powerful, now. Like I have more agency. I can go out and get what I want. I've never felt like this before."

"What did you feel like before?"

"Like a lost little girl. A child with no experience in ... anything, really. Powerless. Like I was at the mercy of the world. Now I feel like I can change the world."

Becks is nodding. "Power is intoxicating. Add some earth-shattering orgasms to the mix, and it's a recipe for..."

"For what?" I ask.

She shakes her head. "I don't know. Obsession?"

I think of Alistair's body, his laugh, his eyes. "Oh, I'm definitely obsessed. Luckily, it seems to be mutual."

CHAPTER 16
Schrödinger Cat

ALISTAIR

Sleep doesn't come easy. Every time I turn over, my body screams in pain. My muddled brain dreams of Ivy; of her softness, her joy, the squeaky clean feel of her skin in the shower. God, what I wouldn't do to have a warm shower.

I don't waste time on feeling sorry for myself. The injuries will heal. The mission remains the same: get the fuck out of here as soon as possible.

The door creaks open, allowing just a sliver of light from the next room. My muscles tense in readiness, which hurts like hell. Is it Arkadi, back to finish what he started? I don't have the strength to defend myself.

No, it's Anya. She sweeps in silently, swaying her hips, smelling of Baccarat Rouge. Her cream and gold shift dress glints. Again, I think of her as an angel—she's pale, clean, and expensive-looking—and I am all dried blood, grit, and grime. We are the perfect foils for each other. She comes right up to me, her nose twitching at my condition, and hands over a cool bottle of water. Without thanking her, I grab it and gulp it down, not bothering to ration myself.

"You poor man," she purrs.

I don't need her pity. I stay quiet.

"Arkadi should not have done this to you."

I flinch when she touches my cheek with something cold. I'm pretty sure the bone is fractured, if not worse.

"Ssh. You're okay. Let me clean you up a little."

I turn away. I don't want her touching any part of me—don't want her evil leaking into me—but we both know that she is in charge.

Still, I resist, and I see the muscles in her jaw clench.

She forces a smile. "If you're good, I'll let you have the painkillers I brought with me."

That's a deal I can live with. I turn back to her, reminding myself of a recalcitrant child bribed with candy.

Anja wipes the specks of dried blood off my face and inspects my other injuries. My six-pack is scabbed and mottled with bruising, and I'm sure my back is in a similar condition.

"It could have been worse," she comments.

"Yes," I deadpan. "I could be dead."

She smirks. "Exactly."

We both know that her intervention is the only reason I'm alive. Well, to be fair, she's also the reason I was in danger in the first place, so there's that. I'm her Schrödinger cat.

Anya twists the cap off a cheap plastic pill bottle that rattles in her perfectly-manicured hand. She spills two tablets into my palm, and passes me another bottle of water. She's clearly feeling generous today.

"You'll get more later, if you behave."

"That should be easy." I wasn't going anywhere in this train-wreck of a body.

Anya doesn't leave.

"What do you want from me?" I rasp.

"You have nothing I want."

"I see. You go around randomly kidnapping people off yachts for no reason."

Anya's eyes turn to ice. "You tried to destroy my family."

I snort a mirthless chuckle. "Only the fucking Russian Bratva would be so arrogant to believe that."

"You deny it? Trying to assassinate my father, blow up my mother?"

"You're being deliberately obtuse, playing the victim here. We both know it's bullshit. You came after us first." How did she think it would go? "Did you expect us *not* to defend ourselves?"

"Ah," Anya crosses her arms. "You think we targeted you randomly. Out of all the most powerful crime families in the whole world, we chose the gilded Ravenscrofts. *Now* who is the arrogant one?"

That stops me short. I had believed that; I believed it was bad luck that the Kuznetsovs had set their sights on us. I hate the smugness in her expression as she laps up my surprise. I feel like an idiot. I had been so wrapped up in Ivy that I had dropped my guard. Of course they chose our family for a reason. Yes, they wanted to use our distribution network, but it's not like the Granite Line is the only uninspected express freight train in the world.

I search her eyes for a clue.

"It was by invitation," Anya says.

My brain can't make sense of that. "What?"

She turns to leave. "That's all you need to know, for now."

This is a different kind of torture. I grit out the words. "An *invitation?*"

Anya gives me that smug smile again, the pursed red lips, and leaves.

CHAPTER 17

Fitful

IVY

When Becks takes my wineglass from me, switching it with a mug of chamomile and sending me to bed, I'm grateful.

My mouth stretches wide with a barely concealed yawn. "You're a true friend," I say.

"Well, someone has to be the grownup around here. Plus, I promised the strict nurse of yours that I'd make sure you got enough rest."

"Bless you."

"Indeed. I hope the gods are listening."

She shepherds me to the spare room, which is simple and cosy. The white cotton bed linen looks so inviting.

"Perfect," I say. "Thank you."

I sink down into the bed without even taking my clothes off. The cool clean sheets are a balm to my nervous body. As soon as my head hits the pillow I feel my looping anxious thoughts grow less demanding. There will be plenty of time to worry tomorrow.

Thank god Becks is here. I'm even glad Noah is here, so that Becks has someone to look after her. I must remember to pay their hotel bill. It's the least I can do.

You're going to be okay, Alistair, I think. *I need you. Baby Alex needs you. I don't know where you are, or how you are, but you're going to be okay.*

It has to be true, because I won't be able to live in a world without him.

I sink into a fitful sleep.

When Alistair comes to me, I know it's a dream. His presence doesn't fool me; nor does the breathtaking view of the sea. I don't care that it's not real. Having him with me, even as a sleepy hallucination, is comforting. We're still in Koh Samui. There are swaying palm trees and snatches of blue sky. The smell of coconut. He's not in one of his beautifully tailored dark suits, but in a loose linen shirt that shows off his new tan.

"God, you're beautiful," he drawls, taking my hips in his hands and pulling me casually toward him. His actions are languorous, but his eyes tell a different story. His gaze is fiercely hungry, like teeth on my skin.

"This is a dream," I say, but he doesn't hear me.

His lips are on my collarbone, firm enough not to tickle. "I want you," he murmurs into my skin.

I push myself into him; my wordless consent. I want him, too. I want every part of him, every inch of his warm, vital body, every breath.

"I wish you were here," I say. He can't hear me in this dream. It's a one-way conversation, if you don't count what our bodies are doing.

We're out on the deck of the private villa. Memories of carefree pleasure paint every surface. The banter, the cocktails, the intense pleasure. Not just the hedonism of the holiday, but the wholesomeness, too. Seeing baby Alex on the beach for the first time, how his face lit up at the magical ocean, the feel of the golden sand, like powder in his hands. Brumilde overseeing us all like a happy aunt.

The loss is visceral.

No, I correct myself, even in a dream.

Not loss. Nothing is lost yet.

Alistair will come back to me.

His hands tighten on my hips; I think he will kiss me, but instead he spins me around and pushes me over the back of the outdoor couch. He's rough now, and I revel in it. The rougher the better, strong and solid, because it's the only way I'll feel anything in this flighting, dreamy moment.

He impatiently jams his fingers inside me, shocking but welcome.

"So wet," he groans into my ear.

The pleasure is murky. I can't really feel it, but I know it's there—or, at least, the idea of it is there. Alistair's hands are always magical, drawing out the best of me.

He gets rougher, pushing me into the furniture and fucking me with his fingers. It awakens something feral in me. I lift my ass as high as it will go—an invitation for him to go as hard and deep as he can.

"This pussy," he whispers, withdrawing his fingers and spanking me.

I want his cock so badly that I whimper for it. I reach back to stroke my clit, finding the area so drenched that I gasp.

"Please fuck me," I beg, even though I know he can't hear me in this strange, surreal world of shifting images and feelings. I want to be filled up by his glorious cock, want it to stretch me wide and pound me deep. Only Alistair's cock can do it right. I want to worship it, suck it, come all over it.

"I love coming on your cock," I tell him. It's my favorite thing.

Alistair spanks me again, exactly where I like it. I imagine the skin there growing pink. I want him inside me so badly.

"Please, Alistair." Growing impatient, I turn my head to look at him, but he catches me and forces me down again. Yes.

He pushes halfway into me, hissing with pleasure. I moan and squirm. It feels so good, the way he stretches me.

"Yes," I moan. "Yes, yes, yes."

He pushes in deeper, and already my body threatens to implode. I guess orgasms come easier in dreams.

I'm holding my boobs with one hand, squeezing a nipple, while I use my other hand to brace myself against the couch as Alistair starts pounding in earnest. It feels good, but too dreamy. I need the real thing.

"Harder," I say. I want everything he can give me.

I focus my attention on his cock, otherwise the sensation just disappears and the dream threatens to float away.

"Harder-harder-harder." I don't want to lose him. "Stay with me, Alistair," I beg.

He drives his hard cock into me over and over again, his breath coming in ragged bursts. I feel my pleasure mount. Yes, it's here.

"Alistair," I cry, as the wave of erotic bliss engulfs me.

He thrusts hard and fast into the pulses of my orgasm, the best feeling in the world, making me come again—and then again.

"Fu-u-u-uck," I cry, and it ends in a sob that breaks the fabric of the dream. Suddenly I'm back in the dark bedroom, alone in a strange bed, sheets tangled around my legs.

I feel completely bereft; the grief hits me like a punch in the stomach.

The sobbing doesn't stop.

CHAPTER 18
Woozy & Warm

ALISTAIR

An invitation.

An invitation to blow up our lives.

I'll go mad not knowing what the fuck Anya meant. I attempt to tell myself that it doesn't matter. That nothing matters except getting out of here and back to Ivy. I need to be with my family to protect them.

But it does matter. Someone invited evil into our family, and they will pay for it. Anya's not going to tell me who it was, so it'll be up to me to find out. With Blackwood gone, our intelligence has flatlined—unless you count the new kid, Brodie. He has yet to prove himself, but if Blackwood was grooming him as a protégé, he must have something unique. Blackwood, may he rest in peace, was fastidious in all his hires, from his au pair to his investment banker. No one unqualified got anywhere near his selection process.

My thoughts turn muddy, my consciousness starts unspooling.

Woozy and warm.

Damn. What was in those painkillers?

Usually, I would fight any lapse in consciousness. It'll make me too vulnerable.

But there's no fighting these meds. It feels like I've main-lined a horse tranquilizer.

The intense pain that wracks my broken body is evaporating, steaming off my skin like smoke. My intercostals, before so tense with pain signals from the broken ribs, relax into comfort. My cheekbone glows as if it is being healed in real time. I sink lower and lower, my lips becoming slack, every muscle of my body relaxing into a slow swirl of near oblivion. My thirst and hunger disappear. The pain is completely gone. It's such a relief as I melt into the mattress.

Ivy appears. Of course she does. She's always there for me when I need her.

"Alistair," she says.

"Ivy." It's so good to see her alive and well. I couldn't ask for anything else. The warmth flows through me.

"Alistair, you can't take the pills again."

At first, I'm so out of it that I don't know what she's talking about. Then I remember the painkillers; the cheap-looking plastic bottle that rattled in Anya's hand.

"I need them. They feel so good," I say.

"Too good," she replies. "That's why you can't take them again."

"So much pain," I argue. "I'm broken."

"No. You're not broken."

"Broken bones…" I say.

"Your bones will heal. You're still the man you've always been. You'll get out of this and we'll be together again."

I nod, desperate to believe it. "Yes."

"…But not if you keep taking the pills. Do you understand?"

I nod again. The pills are not the way out of this. If anything, they'll keep me here, pinned to this mattress, lost in oblivion.

"Yes."

Ivy looks pleased. She smiles, and her eyes sparkle. "I can't wait till we're together again."

She hoists her skirt up and straddles me, stroking my cock as she moves against me in her panties. I don't see her take her clothes off, but now she's naked apart from small cotton undies, and I watch her thrusting on top of me, rolling her hips, her beautiful breasts moving in a way that makes me want to fuck them.

"Ivy," I say. "So beautiful. So goddamn perfect."

She grins, enjoying putting on the show for me. "I'm just a fantasy."

"You're just as perfect in real life."

The room starts to spin, and I'm battling to keep my eyes open.

"Stay with me," she urges. "Don't give in to the darkness."

I force my eyes to stay open, but they want to close again almost immediately.

My mouth is so dry I can hardly talk. I want to stay with her, stay with the light, but everything is fading.

"Look at me," Ivy commands.

I prize my lids open. I don't remember closing them.

Ivy smiles again, touching her tits, which are now encased in a sexy-as-fuck black mesh corset. She's rubbing against me, and it feels so good I think I'll start floating.

Maybe I'm already floating.

I'm too numb to get hard, but a sweet vortex of pleasure whirls where Ivy is touching me. I don't need to be hard. I don't need anything. I have Ivy.

"Promise me," she says, still moving in that magnificent way, breasts swaying. I want to suck her nipples.

I shake my head to clear it.

Promise what?

Where am I?

"Promise me you won't take the pills again."

"Yes," I reply, my consciousness buzzing like a lightbulb about to die.

"Say it."

"I promise I won't take the pills."

"Good." She bears down harder, as a reward, and I moan.

I find the edge of her panties—they're back to being the simple cotton briefs—and push my fingers inside her. She's dripping wet.

I groan again. "Fuck. I love the way you feel."

Ivy's thrusting slowly, head thrown back. Her muscles squeeze my fingers.

"You have to come back to me, Alistair. We've got so much to discover."

I want to reply, but I'm melting again. Losing myself. Disappearing into the darkness.

"Come back to me, Alistair," she says, but I am gone.

CHAPTER 19
Multiple Threats

IVY

I awake with a jolt. There is shouting. My heart hammers, threatening to tear through my chest. An angry male voice triggers my PTSD, and I break into a cold sweat thinking of Jeff, even though I know he's dead. I lie frozen in place, breath coming in short gasps.

It must be Noah shouting.

Is Noah shouting at Becks? *How dare he!*

I wrench the sheets aside, almost tripping in my haste to get to my friend. I freeze when I get to the door, recognizing the accent of the shouter. The *Irish* accent.

Not Noah, but Henderson.

My anger dissipates. Of course he's here, and of course he's angry. I no longer want to open the door. I don't want to face his fury. Guilt and shame pushes me back.

"What the FUCK were you thinking?" he's demanding.

"She was all alone in a hospital. In a foreign country!" yells Becks in reply. "I was thinking I could take care of her better here."

"You risked her life. Anything could have happened. They could have followed you. Abducted her. *Killed her.*"

Becks lowers her voice. It's muffled, but I can still make it out. "Is this really about Ivy?"

Silence.

"Of course it's about bloody Ivy. What else would it be about?"

"You don't seem too happy about the fact that I came here with a man."

"Well, yeah. Don't get me started on that. It's like you tried to introduce multiple threats at once."

"Noah isn't a threat," she counters.

"Anyone who hasn't been thoroughly vetted by our intelligence is a threat, Rebecca."

"Does that include me?"

"It includes you most of all, after this. We can no longer trust you to do what is in Ivy's best interest."

"Oh, fuck off."

"I'd be happy to!" he yells. "Except that you've now complicated this in such a way that I can't leave without Ivy. And my main priority right now should be looking for Alistair, not cleaning up your bloody mess."

I feel terrible. I push open the bedroom door. "I'm really sorry, Henderson."

His face softens, as does his tone. "Ah, would you look now. It's not your fault, Ivy."

Seeing me in the doorway, most probably looking pale and shaky, takes the wind out of his sails. He slumps down on the couch and rubs his face, as if he is trying to straighten out his thoughts.

"Can I make you a coffee?" I offer.

Becks, face pink with anger and perhaps a tinge of guilt, huffs and stamps into the kitchenette. "I'll make the fucking coffee."

I pad over and sit next to Henderson.

"I am really sorry. I didn't mean to add to your worries."

He shakes his head. He's well known in the security team for not needing sleep to function, but I see dark circles under his eyes, and his concern is etched all over his unusually downcast face.

"It's not your fault," he echoes. "Not your fault I can't find Alistair."

He inhales deeply through his nose and looks at the ceiling.

Tears spring to my eyes. Seeing stoical Henderson like this makes me so full of fear and dread that I want to vomit. I swallow a few times before I can talk.

"What do we know?" I whisper.

"Nothing," he replies, rubbing the stubble on his chin. "Absolutely fuck all. We're hoping they'll make contact now that the family is here."

Of course, the Ravenscrofts arrived in Thailand last night.

"Brodie advised them to come over. In case there are negotiations to be had."

"Brodie?" I ask.

"The new intelligence agent. Blackwood's protégé. May he rest in peace."

Henderson signs the holy trinity. I never knew he was religious. Maybe he's not. Maybe it's just muscle memory from childhood, or an anxious tic.

"Of course," I reply. "He seems good."

Henderson shrugs. "Alistair trusts him, so that's good enough for me."

Becks, tight-lipped and sulky, slams hot mugs on the table before us, then makes herself scarce by having her coffee outside on the balcony, her bare feet up on the railing. Henderson pulls his eyes away from her.

"You can't stay here," he says. "I know you want to, but you can't."

I gulp. "I understand."

"You'll stay with us. With the family. We've taken the Fronds Hotel."

We've taken the Fronds Hotel—I assume that means they've hired out the entire building for privacy.

I don't want to stay at a fancy hotel. I don't want to stay here, either. I'm craving our house with Reacher, Bijou, Brumilde, and baby Alex. The fireplace and the bedroom. Alistair. Tears sting my eyes again.

Alistair.

Henderson sees my distress, and his spine straightens. I see resolve in his expression.

"We're gonna find him," he promises me, eyes glinting with determination.

I shoot Becks a look of apology as we leave.

She grips my shoulders. "It's the right thing to do. You'll be safer with Henderson. I'm not going anywhere. I'll be here when you need me."

"Thank you," I whisper into her hair as we hug goodbye.

Henderson and Becks have a final stare-down.

"I'll send you Ivy's number when we grab her a new phone," he says. "If you promise not to kidnap her again."

"Ah, sod off," she says, but there is a reluctant smile in her eyes.

Henderson spots the bottle of champagne on the counter as we leave. "Did Noah bring this?"

"Yes," replies Becks. "Why?"

"Good," says Henderson, swiping it.

Becks opens her mouth, but Henderson doesn't wait to hear what she has to say.

CHAPTER 20
The Poison She's Peddling

ALISTAIR

When I wake up, I feel like I've been hit by a bus. Granted, being beaten by Arkadi is probably as destructive as being flattened by a red double-decker—but it's not just my body that's sore. My head's about to explode with the worst hangover I've ever experienced. I guess horse tranquilizers will do that to you, or whatever the fuck Anya dosed me with. Some kind of vicious street opioid. Jesus Christ. The room is still spinning. I swallow the vomit that climbs up my throat. Whatever it was, I know it was evil, because despite feeling so ill, I want more of it.

It's dangerous and addictive—my dream of Ivy made sure I knew it. Now, I just need the willpower to resist the oblivion it provides. I've never been tempted to try hard drugs; I like to feel in control. Especially in a situation like this, where I need to be sharp and agile. No more happy dust for me, no matter how much I want the relief.

The hours drag by, and the ache at my temple worsens. My skull is in a vise. It turns out that the pills hadn't taken away the pain after all, just funneled it into my head. It gets worse and worse, until I want it all to end. I find myself not caring about anything but stopping the pain. Instead of fantasizing about Ivy, I dream of a loaded revolver. I think of how good the cold metal of the barrel would feel against my temple; of how I'll squeeze the trigger and explode into nothing.

I must have passed out, because when I open my eyes again, Anya is staring at me. I flinch, and move back, trying to put some distance between us, but all I manage to do is push further into my pillow. My brain is pounding against my skull, and the nausea has returned.

"You poor thing," she croons, reaching out to touch my forehead.

I want to swat her hand away, but my limbs seem to be made out of lead.

I don't want her anywhere near me. Her or that poison she's peddling.

"I brought you some food," she says. "Water. And more painkillers."

I think of Ariana and how she was slowly manipulated into thinking that her captors were her benefactors. That won't happen to me. But I do need food. Apart from the gnawing feeling in my gut that is a constant companion, I need energy to be able to fight, and protein to heal. And water. God, I need water. I'm so parched that it hurts to swallow.

As if reading my mind, she passes me a dripping bottle. It's cold and slippery with condensation, and feels good in my palm. She taps out the pills, and I pretend to swallow them along with some water, tucking the tablets into my curled fingers. She wants me weak. Dependent on her. No matter what games she plays, it's never going to happen. I gulp down the water, squeezing the bottle as if my life depended on it. I hate the desperation of it all, but true thirst will do that to you.

"I have disciplined Arkadi," she announces, pretending to be on my side.

I flick my gaze up to look at her. She's completely out of place here in her designer clothes, the grime all around us forcing her pale, expensive outfit into stark contrast. The only clue that she belongs here is the hint of a gun holstered on her thigh.

"He shouldn't have beaten you so badly. He has been punished."

I don't reply. How does one discipline a man like Arkadi? Like a mountain, he seems unpunishable. Whichever way she did it, I'm certain that Arkadi wants me dead more than ever.

"But," she drawls, "you are the one who tried to escape. If you hadn't done that, Arkadi wouldn't have hurt you. So, you ... also need to be punished."

I find my current situation punishment enough, but it looks like she has other plans.

Fuck my life.

I need to get the fuck out of here. Where is my team? Where the fuck is Henderson? Blackwood would have found me by now, but now I seem to be employing his bloody teenage intern.

Anya digs in the pocket of her elegant cream blazer and pulls out something that glints in the low light; metallic and sharp. A knife. Some sort of fucking Russian dagger. Involuntarily, I push back into the pillow again. My body reacts instinctively, like a whipped dog when its abuser holds up their hand.

"We're not going to struggle," she instructs, her eyes glittering like the blade. "You're going to take your punishment like a man, and then you can have your dinner."

Her excited expression terrifies me. Before, I regarded her as a cold-blooded killer, but now I see that she's a sadist, and that's a lot scarier. Cold-blooded killers don't enjoy the hunt or the kill; it's just a necessary part of the job. Sadists, however—

She bites her bottom lip and brings the dagger up to my face. What will she do? Disfigure me so that I look like one of her scarred thugs? Or, much worse, gouge an eye out?

What did she do to Arkadi?

I bite down, willing my body to stay still. I want to fight. I want to grab her gun, or snatch the blade and turn it on her. I wouldn't think twice about plunging it into her neck —I'd be doing the world a favor.

I grit my teeth so hard that the pain from my fractured cheekbone shears through me. I wince but hold my groan in.

Do not fight.

Do not fight.

Do not fight.

There will be a time to defend and to retaliate, but this is not it. Not if I want to get out of here alive. Not if I ever want to see Ivy again.

She smiles at me. It's a satisfied smirk that she can see my pain and fear laid bare. For a second I think she is bluffing, that she only wanted to see me stricken, but then she does it. The blade slices my skin so quickly and neatly that it makes me wonder if she's done any damage at all.

I feel the warm blood dripping before I feel the sting of it, but when the pain arrives, it's brutal. I clutch at my ear, shocked and gasping.

"Give me your shirt," she says. She's calm, the way psychopaths are.

A wave of dizziness shunts me back, but I obey her, pulling the blood-stained T-shirt over my head and passing it to her.

"Thank you." She's indifferent, as if we had just completed an everyday transaction. As if she's not sitting there with a dagger and a bloody rag in her hands.

CHAPTER 21
Balls of Steel

IVY

Henderson and I arrive at the fancy Fronds hotel and are immediately swept up into the elevator and into the luxurious penthouse suite. I am no longer shocked by opulence, but it did look ridiculously big and insanely decked out. There was just so much ... space. And light.

Shiny copper fittings and bright, bold tropical print wallpaper give it added charm. Classical music blares from concealed speakers.

"Your bedroom's down that hall," says Henderson, nodding to the left.

"Oh," I murmur, "surely they'll want their space. I'll get a small single room downstairs."

Meaning, of course, that I'd be more comfortable in my own room. As much affection as I had for the Ravenscrofts,

I didn't want to bunk with them, penthouse or not. And, given my state of mind, I could do with some time alone.

"Nonsense!" scolds Isobel, rounding the corner and opening her arms wide to hug me. "You *must* stay with us. I'll go mad otherwise!"

I let her envelop me. It's comforting to be hugged by a mum, even if she's not, strictly speaking, mine. I blink away my tears.

She takes me by the shoulders. "Banish those tears, dear. We don't need them. Alistair certainly doesn't need them."

Christopher ambles in. He's wearing a flamboyant silk dressing robe that shimmers as he walks. "Oh, it's the vegan."

I'm used to his digs now, and don't bother correcting him. He's teasing me but there is warmth in his voice.

"Drink?" he offers. "I must warn you, there's no decent champagne in the country, but the vodka is passable."

I look pointedly at the large clock on the wall. I'm all for a good vodka tonic, but it's not even ten a.m.

He shrugs. "I'm still on British time."

"Of *course* you'll stay with us," reiterates Isobel. "We need you here."

Christopher clears his throat. *Speak for yourself,* his body language says.

"*I* need you here," she insists. "Otherwise, I just have these ... barbarians ... for company."

Henderson pretends to be offended.

"Oh, not you dear," she quickly says, then points her thumb at her silk-robed son.

She said barbarians, plural, so I'm guessing Mr Ravenscroft is here, too, but I don't think the man had a barbaric bone in his body—not anymore, anyway. Although the music is quite loud.

"Where are your things?" Isobel asks. "Is the porter bringing them up?"

"Er," I say.

"Mother," laughs Christopher. "She was pushed off a fucking yacht in the middle of the ocean. What did you expect her to bring? A shipwreck fork to comb her hair?"

"Language," warns Isobel.

I stare at him. "Did you just reference a *Disney* movie?"

"What?" he demands, apparently deeply affronted. "You're too good for Disney?"

"No," I reply, "I'm just surprised, that's all."

"Surprised that barbarians can appreciate 'The Little Mermaid'?"

"I'm not the one who called you a barbarian," I say.

Isobel gets a wistful look on her face. "They used to love watching that film, all three of them." And she promptly bursts into tears.

"What happened to not crying?" says Christopher gently, coming forward and hugging his mum. She looks so small and vulnerable suddenly. "It's okay. It's going to be okay. You know what Alistair is like. He'll be fine."

I don't like the way his voice wobbles at the end. The lump in my throat grows bigger.

"I'll make coffee," Henderson says.

Once we all have a steaming mug in our hands, thanks to Henderson, we sit down for the debrief. Isobel has recovered—and is clearly wearing top-quality waterproof mascara because she still looks as flawless as always. Thankfully, she managed to convince Gregory to turn the blaring music down, but he hasn't yet joined us for the meeting.

"Will we wait for Mr Ravenscroft?" Henderson asks.

Isobel shakes her head. "This incident has set him back. Finding Ariana was good for him, but he's not taking this ... latest development very well. No parent should have to deal with this kind of worry."

"And look at you," says Christopher, admiration in his tone. "You're as strong as ever. You've always had balls of steel."

I look at Isobel, perfectly made up, elegant in her stylish suit, and inwardly agree with Christopher. Balls of steel, indeed.

"What's the point of a debrief when there's no new information?" asks Christopher.

Henderson rubs his chin and sets his mug down. "Because we need a plan. We've exhausted our leads. The team needs direction."

"We need to throw everything we have at it," states Chris. "The cops, the private investigators, the fucking Thai army. I don't care what it costs. We'll check every fucking house and shack in the country."

"We aren't certain if he's in the country," admits Henderson. "He could be in Norilsk for all we know."

"But he's alive," says Christopher.

"There's no evidence to suggest otherwise," Henderson replies.

"He's alive," I say. "I can feel it."

Christopher has to have a go at me. "You can *feel* it? So, you're what? Clairvoyant now? Alistair's dating a vegan psychic. Who would have guessed?"

"I know you're under stress, dear," says Isobel firmly, "but I won't have you taking it out on Ivy. She's been nothing but clever and brave since this whole debacle began. Do I have to remind you who saved Ariana's life when she was shot? And, in doing so, also saved the life of my grandchild?"

This makes me frown. With all the drama lately, I had forgotten that Ariana was pregnant.

"Where are Brumilde and Alex?" I ask, suddenly afraid for them.

"Resting," says Isobel, a smile returning to her face. "Safe and warm, here in the suite."

I feel a deep need to cuddle Alex. I didn't realize how much I had missed him.

Henderson's phone buzzes, and he snatches it up.

"A message from Brodie," he tells us. A dark look looms on his face, which makes my insides clench and my heart race.

"What is it?" I whisper.

Henderson blanches. "He's phoning with news. He said to prepare ourselves."

CHAPTER 22
Dead Bodies Don't Bleed

IVY

Prepare ourselves?

What the fuck!

No, no, no.

"Let's keep calm," says Henderson. "Whatever it is, the information may move us forward."

"He would have said," gulps Christopher. "He would have said if they had found the body."

"Yes," Henderson agrees. "He certainly would have."

Chris gets up to grab the bottle of vodka, then sits back down again.

It's obviously bad news. You don't tell a worried family to

prepare themselves if it's good news. You just blurt out the good news.

The phone in Henderson's hand starts buzzing. Even though he was expecting the call, he fumbles and almost drops it. I would have done the same.

I'm desperate to know what the news is, and equally desperate to shut it out.

Christopher's words comfort me.

He would have said if they had found the body.

"You're on speaker," Henderson says.

"Hello, it's Brodie here," says Blackwood's protégé.

Christopher sighs and rolls his eyes at the intern stating the obvious. His subtext is clear — *THIS is who we're trusting with my brother's life??*

I ignore him and focus on my breathing. *Yoga*, I think desperately. I need to do yoga to stay sane. My whole body is stiff with fear. I'm so brittle I'll shatter if I fall.

"Yeah, we know, Brodie," says Henderson. "Tell us what's happened."

"This is going to be difficult to hear," he begins. "I hope you're all sitting—"

"For fuck's sake, man!" yells Christopher. "Spit it out! Is my brother alive?"

"We believe so," replies Brodie, apparently unoffended by Christopher's cursing.

I scrunch my eyes shut.

Thank you god.

Thank you universe.

Thank you thank you thank you.

A sob rises in my throat, but I push it down. I need to hear the rest.

I steal a look at Isobel, who is clutching at her chest. I want to tell her to breathe.

Henderson sounds cautiously optimistic. "That sounds positive. Tell us what you have."

It's Brodie's turn to take a breath. We hear him sigh. My stomach knots again.

"We received a ... *parcel* from the Mirror Bratva an hour ago. A black gift box with a ribbon. I was pretty sure it was an explosive device—given the Fabergé incident—so I took extra time to ascertain that it wasn't dangerous before opening it."

"Go on," prods Henderson.

I ignore my instinct to run away. I force myself to stay and listen.

"It's important to note that we haven't had the tissue tested yet."

"What?" demands Christopher. "What *tissue*? What is he on about?"

Isobel shushes him so that she can hear what Brodie has to say.

"The blood is his. It's Alistair's DNA."

"What?" I gasp. "What is he saying?"

"It was an ear," says Brodie. "I'm really sorry."

I hear Henderson swallow. "To be clear. The Bratva sent you an ... *ear*."

"Correct," Brodie confirms. "And a shirt. The blood was mostly on the shirt."

"It's definitely his blood?" asks Isobel. "Alistair's blood?"

"No doubt there," says Brodie. "I'm sorry."

I crumple. I want to lie on the floor, but I'm frozen. My beautiful Alistair, what have they done to you?

"This is excellent news," states Isobel, and we all look at her as if she's completely lost the plot.

Christopher clears his throat. "Um, mother?"

She puts her hand up. "Now, I know it's terrible. What was in the box."

I realize I'm rocking myself gently, trying to keep calm.

"But he's ALIVE. Dead bodies don't bleed. Isn't that so, Brodie?"

"Correct, Mrs Ravenscroft," he replies. "Whilst this is disturbing, I do think it's a positive sign. Alistair's alive and kicking."

Alive and *bleeding,* I think. But, still, they're right. As shocking as this is, the most important thing is that he's alive. I nod. I tap my knee. I look at Isobel. Yes. This is good news. If I say it enough times, perhaps I'll believe it.

"What did the note say?" asks Henderson. "What do they want?"

"There was no note. While I don't like to assume anything, ever, my thinking is that they want what they've always wanted," says Brodie. "Unfettered access to our distribution network."

"With a side dish of revenge," says Christopher.

"If they can use the Granite line it opens up vast business opportunities for them," says Brodie. "And the daughter, Anya, is all about business."

"She was the one on the yacht," I add, unhelpfully. Everyone knew that already.

"I don't believe a word," utters Isobel. "It's not about *business.* It may have started that way, but we're too far down the rabbit hole now to ever work together. They took 'business' off the table when they tried to murder us in our own home."

"Yeah," snorts Christopher. "Business Relationships 101: Don't try to kill your network."

"They'll know we're not open to working with them," says Isobel. "So why even ask?"

"Because they are arrogant, stubborn, and they have the biggest bargaining chip of all," replies Christopher.

"I think we all know that a business relationship won't be sustainable in the long term," says Brodie. "Or even the short term."

"But they have Alistair," I say.

"Yes," says Brodie. "But they have Alistair."

I think I might vomit. I clutch my stomach.

"There's another small nugget of good news," says Brodie.

Oh, god. Another wave of anxiety hits me. Brodie's good news seems to come in the form of severed body parts. I brace myself.

"We picked up a partial print on the underside of the box."

"So what?" asks Christopher. "We already know who sent it."

"Because it wasn't a Kuznetsov print?" guesses Henderson.

"Correct," says Brodie. "Delivery guy. A Koh Samui local."

Isobel sits up. "Can you trace it back to where he collected it from?"

"We're trying," says Brodie. "At this point, any intel is golden. One partial might be all it takes."

I breathe out slowly. This is going better than expected. My urge to be sick and/or lie on the floor has given way to a small spark of hope.

"I'll let you know the moment I hear back on the labs," the intern says.

Henderson thanks him and ends the call. "We may need to negotiate on Granite," he says. "Are we willing to entertain that?"

"I'm willing to negotiate anything for my son's life," replies Isobel, "but I can tell you right now that we can't do business with these people. It'll never work."

Christopher takes a slug of vodka straight out of the bottle. "So, we agree to their terms, then deal with the fallout later?"

Isobel shakes her head. "It's a non-starter. It makes absolutely zero sense. But, yes. What else can we do?"

"Probably more about the revenge, then," muses Chris. "But then why are they keeping Alistair alive?"

"He's more valuable alive than dead," says Henderson.

"None of it makes sense," I say. "Is there perhaps something we haven't thought of?"

Christopher rubs his face. "Probably. In my case, most definitely."

I'm not used to him being self-deprecating. I smile at him, despite the circumstances. Despite the feeling I have that the Kuznetsovs won't stop at anything until we're all dead.

Alex's whimpering reaches us, and I jump up. "I'll go."

I hotfoot it down a wide passage, following the sad sound. When I see him standing in his travel cot, my heart expands and tears prick my eyes.

"Alex!" I whisper, not wanting to wake Brumilde, who is napping. "Baby!" I get all choked up. "I've missed you so much!"

His eyes widen, and he smiles when he sees me. He even does a little bounce of happiness on his chunky little legs. Brumilde's been feeding him well.

"Hello, chonks," I say. "I think you've grown since I last saw you a few days ago."

He raises his arms, and I pick him up. He does another little jig against me, and I chuckle. Tears are streaming down my face.

"Oh, baby. I have missed you. Shall we go and get a snack? There's a fancy little snack bar in this fancy penthouse. Did you know that? Are you even allowed snacks? I don't know these things yet. You'll have to teach me." I keep babbling to him, hoping it makes him feel safe despite my deluge of tears. "Or maybe you want a nice warm bottle. Millie's sleeping, so I can make you one. You know, your uncle Christopher also likes his bottle."

CHAPTER 23
Struggle

ALISTAIR

I'm gathering the courage to attempt to escape again. I can't stand being so vulnerable. I need to get out of here. I have six pills saved up now; you never know when they'll come in handy as a weapon, or, probably more likely, as an easy way out if it gets too much to bear. They tempt me constantly with their promise of oblivion.

My body is healing. The incision on my ear took its time to stop bleeding, but is now scabbed over. For the moment, this is a mental game. I must not lose hope or focus.

I keep reminding myself of the reasons I can't die in here.

I take a deep breath and try to bring Ivy to life in my imagination, real and present, like she had been in my dream. I swear I could actually touch her. I could feel her warmth. I would do anything to feel her skin again.

Eyes closed, I think of her incredible smile, the one that melts me every time. Her breasts, the skin soft as silk as I put my face between them. The way they move, so feminine and delicious. Her nipples that harden on my tongue.

Okay, she's here. I have her. I have conjured her up.

Ivy.

Relief, but also arousal.

God, she's beautiful.

"I need you," I say. I hate how weak I sound.

She doesn't seem to mind, she just smiles and kisses me.

This vision of Ivy doesn't seem to talk, so I'll get my fix of her in other ways. I run my fingers through her hair, put my thumb on her bottom lip. She smiles and takes it into her mouth, warm and soft. My cock wakes up as she gently sucks my thumb.

Ivy doesn't break eye contact. Her expression is saying that I can do whatever I want to her; take whatever I need. Like the time in the hospital when Ariana was in trouble and I didn't know what to do with myself. Ivy knew what I needed. An uncomplicated rough fuck in a strange room.

Ivy has the ability to settle me in a way I can't do myself. Her grounded energy, generous spirit, incredible heart, and welcoming body. If I'm honest, it's the welcoming body I want now.

I wouldn't do it exactly the same way as we did in the hospital. I'd start slow this time and build up. I'd trace the back of her neck with my finger, raising goosebumps, then slowly unbutton her dress.

I realize, with surprise, that I don't want her to be a supplicant in this fantasy. I want her to fight a bit.

I frown. This is new to me. Consent has always been a priority.

But somehow this fantasy version of Ivy has agreed to this. A little bit of a struggle—because I need it. I swallow the uncertainty I feel. This goes against my primary instinct to always protect her at all costs.

Ivy nods at me. She's saying that I should do what I need to do. When I hesitate, she gently shoves me, like a child signaling they want to play a bit of rough-and-tumble. When I don't take the bait, she pushes me again, harder.

Conflicted, confused by this new desire, I grab her arm. Her expression is all mischief as she tries to get away, but even in this state, I'm so much stronger than her. It's easy to pin her against the wall. Ivy gasps at my forcefulness, and her pupils dilate with desire. She bites her bottom lip and bats her eyelashes at me—the coquettish virgin, nervous about the large erection pushing up against her.

Still playing, she tries to duck away, but I grab her and force her up against the wall again. I rip open her dress, scattering the delicate buttons on the concrete floor. I push down her bra, revealing her perfect tits, and devour them. Ivy is gasping and panting. I bury my hand in her panties, thrusting a finger into her delicious pussy. She tries to keep me out by crossing her legs, but I shove them open and kiss her hard. She gets three fingers for that. When she tries to move away again, I look at her closely to ensure she's still game, and she nods. I spin her around and lift the back of her dress, driving my rock-hard cock inside her without warning. She yells and stretches her fingers out on the wall.

I stop, worried I've hurt her. She reaches back and pulls me closer, thrusting my cock even deeper, and sighs in pleasure. My free hand strums her clit as I rock into her. She is my salvation, all warm soft wet cunt. Fuck. It's too much. It's too good.

I withdraw to catch my breath. When Ivy side-steps me, I push her back and spank her ripe and ready ass. I spank harder and harder, waiting for a cry of pain that doesn't come. She's moaning and her skin begins to glow pink. Fuck, I want to bite her. I sink to my knees and bury my face in her palm-warmed ass, biting and sucking her beautiful swollen cheeks. My fingers travel back to her pussy, so plump and wet that it drives me crazy. They slide in easily, and Ivy squeezes them with her powerful muscles, making me groan with want. Still on my knees, biting and sucking, I begin fucking her with my fingers. She's so juicy it runs down my hand.

"Jesus, Ivy," I mutter. She moans in response; a sound that means she wants more. I stand again, my cock straining for her. I growl into her ear. "You always know what I need."

Hands still on the wall, she pushes out her ass to allow me easy access. My cock wants to explode before it makes it all the way in, but I breathe to ground myself. Coming now will ruin everything; I need to be hard to demolish Ivy in the way I'm craving.

Once I've pulled myself together, I push into her. Ivy's rolling moan tells me everything I need to know. I find her clit with my wet fingers and I thrust myself in as far as I can go. She swallows me up, so tight and slick that I almost lose myself.

"Fu-u-ck," I groan.

Ivy makes one more half-hearted attempt to get away from me, but I grab her and push her back into position, then absolutely launch into her. A darkness possesses me. All the anger and fear inside me drives me into Ivy again and again, hard and deep. My nightmares, my pain. I empty it all into the goddess and she takes it. It's a fevered kind of fucking that I've never experienced before; a violent therapy, full of shadows and taboo. Still, I go harder and faster. I need to get it all out. I need to purge myself of this place, these people, and the terror of no longer being able to protect Ivy or my family. It surges through my body, and this time, I allow it. I come in a storm of pleasure, emptying my darkness into her, knowing that her magical pussy will transform it into light.

CHAPTER 24

Pole

ALISTAIR

The erotic fantasy I had of Ivy energizes me. Yes, I'm still injured, but I can work around that. What's a fractured rib between friends? My broken cheekbone won't stop me from building my strength. I've had years of practice ignoring pain.

I'm going to do whatever it takes to get back to her.

This time when I jump to do pull-ups on the old black pole, something happens. It feels different. I do it again, putting all my body weight on it. The pole moves. It's dim, and I can't easily make out what is happening, but on the third try, a rusted screw breaks off, the head pinging on the concrete floor below.

YES.

Yes, yes, yes.

If one of the screws was rusted through enough to break, then chances are the others are, too.

I can hear my heart beating. This is it.

I spend the next hour pulling the thing down, screw by screw. The first one takes time, but once that pops, the rest take more strain with each pull. Once the left side is done, breaking the last two screws on the right is easy.

Once I have the pole in my hands I feel giddy, like a child with a gift they have yet to unwrap. This is my ticket out of here. Hope, relief, and pain flow through me. I inspect the corner where the pole had been fixed to the wall. It's not obvious that it's missing, because it was pretty much camouflaged before I got it down—a black pole against dark gray bricks and concrete in a dim room.

I've got my ticket out of here, but now I have to wait for one of them to open the door. I sit on the mattress, covering the pole with the grubby blanket. No, that won't work. I stand and tuck it into the back of my waistband. It leans snugly against my back, ready for me to reach around and grab it, like a sword out of a scabbard. If all goes well, they won't see it coming, and I'll be free.

I celebrate by leaning back against the wall and fantasizing about Ivy—about what I'll do to her when we're back together. I think of the play parties I'll take her to, the play-mates we'll meet. I think of long Sunday mornings in bed, me mapping out every square inch of her naked, exquisite body. First with my fingertips, then with my lips. Stroking and massaging and cuddling for days, skin-on-skin. Rubbing warm oil into her back, her tits, her ass. Sucking her clit while I finger her, tracing the shape of her G-spot while she writhes and pants. Then entering her, always such a snug fit, hot and wet, as I grind my cock into her, making sure I reach all the spots that make her crazy. I'll suck her nipples and wind my hands gently around her throat. Never hard enough to hurt her, never. Just to signal who's in charge, the way she likes. The way I make her feel safe. I'll make her come over and over. Intense full-body orgasms that make her lose control and scream. I can't wait to touch her again.

I have a weapon. I have a plan. Soon, I'll be making my way back to Ivy.

CHAPTER 25

The Mosquito and the Mountain

ALISTAIR

This time when Arkadi comes for me, I'm ready. He grunts as he pushes open the heavy metal door. I'm hopped up on nerves and can't help reacting when I see the bandage around his head. He's missing an ear. And, judging by the murderous expression on his face, he blames me for it.

Something tells me that this will be our last confrontation. What I'm not yet certain of is who will survive it.

"Last chance, comrade," I tell him. "I can make you a very rich man. I can keep your family safe. You'll never have to work again. More importantly, you won't have to be on Anya's chopping block anymore."

Arkadi grunts. "The Bratva is my family."

"The kind who cuts off body parts of their family members?"

He doesn't reply. I guess he thinks he deserved the punishment. He did go against Anya's orders, and, judging by the way he looks at her, she's his deity. He disobeyed his god and had to face the brutal consequences. Fucking Soviet sadists.

The only silver lining is that he might not make the same mistake this time.

I haven't moved off the mattress since he arrived. The pipe is still tucked into the back of my waistband. I'll need the element of surprise, given his huge physical advantage over me.

"I need to talk to Anya," I say.

"Mne plevat," he replies. *I don't give a shit.*

He didn't bring food or water. I frown at him. "Why are you here?"

"We're moving locations."

My heart skips a beat. Surely that means my team is close to locating me? I feel my makeshift weapon against my back. A fight will surely be lethal for one of us—probably me—but if Henderson is close, he can get me out of here alive.

Why else would we change locations? It's fraught with risk for them. Then I get a tingle of anxiety down my spine: are we really moving locations, or have they decided it's game over for me? I reach back for the pole, gripping the shaft.

"I'm not going anywhere," I say.

Arkady's expression remains stony. "You don't have to go anywhere. I will take you."

I can imagine him hoisting me over his shoulder.

"I'm staying here," I clarify. "I'm not leaving this room. I've gotten rather attached to the damp stains and plague rats."

"The new place has nicer rats," he says.

"I prefer them feral," I reply.

The moment is surreal — it's almost like Arkadi has a sense of humor. But not quite. He advances on me as if to highlight the point. "Time to go."

"Not until I see Anya," I say.

"Anya's at the new location," he replies.

I think he's bluffing, but his face gives nothing away. I wouldn't want to play poker with the man.

I'm quiet for a while, as if considering it, then move as if I'm about to get up. "Okay," I sigh. "Let's go meet the nice rats."

There is a hint of Arkadi's body relaxing. I take the gap.

Metal pipe in hand, I spring up and bring it down on his skull as hard as I can. The pole vibrates as if I have hit solid rock, which makes me wonder if he even felt it. As my hand hums with the reverb, I see a trickle of blood spill down his forehead and into his eye. He blinks at me and wipes it away, leaving a dramatic red smear down his cheek. Then he comes for me.

The blow would have killed most people, but Arkadi treats it as foreplay. He smiles as he reaches for me, thirsty for vengeance. I try to get a second blow in, but he catches the pipe. I don't let it go. Fuck. This is my chance to run.

Giving Arkadi as wide a berth as possible, I try to get past him, but his arm shoots out like a scrum half reaching for a ball. He just manages to scrag me, but I still have the pole, and I strike him with it as hard as I can, this time smashing the back of his knees. He buckles, but does not fall.

Arkadi grabs me by the shoulders, ready to slam my forehead in what I'm sure would be a lethal head-butt. There is still blood running into his eye, lending him the appearance of a demon. I twist and buck, but I can't wrestle out of his grip. I know that punching him will only result in cracked knuckles. I am a mosquito to his mountain. I'm firmly in his grip and damn dear helpless as he rears back, ready to shatter my skull.

"Arkadi!" yells Anya from the doorway.

I don't look at her; I'm completely transfixed by the orc's monstrous, crimson-painted face, bulging eyes, and desperately bad breath. He's frozen in place, desperate to kill me, but he can't disobey a direct order from his queen. The only movement is the throbbing vein at his temple, and his rippling jaw muscles.

"Arkadi," she says again, her voice icy. She won't warn him again. She may be his deity, but he is her dog, and she's calling him to heel.

He twitches and growls; a dangerous vibration between us as he slowly releases his grip. The second I know I can move, I swing around with all the might I can summon, letting the pipe fly in Anya's direction. She ducks too late. It clocks her right in the face, knocking her to the floor.

Arkadi lets out a primal roar and reaches for me again, but this time I'm ahead of him. I dive onto Anya, snapping her handgun out of the holster. I roll onto my back facing Arkadi, switch the safety off, and fire into his chest.

The first bullet is a mere irritation to him.

I remember Anya calling my rubber-bullet injuries mosquito bites. Again, I am the mosquito.

Two more bullets find their way into his chest, and he's still coming for me. He's an inch away when I finally get him with a headshot. He is falling in my direction, and I need to roll away before he crushes me. His momentum brings him further than I expect. I roll out of his way just in time, but Anya can't. He's dead by the time he lands on her. His leviathan body crushing hers makes an awful sound that I immediately push out of my mind or risk hearing in nightmares for the rest of my life.

You'd think that I would jump up from that cold concrete prison floor and race out of there, but I can't move. Relief overwhelms me, and I am at the same time light as air and pinned to the floor by it. I move my head to look at the corpses lying next to me in their final embrace. I'm exhausted, thirsty as fuck, and so acutely relieved that I have a hard lump in my throat.

It's over.

Only the idea of getting back to Ivy finally gives me the energy to get up. I'm a bit wobbly on my feet, but I manage. Gun in hand, I go in search of water. If there are more people to kill on the way out, I'll consider that a bonus.

CHAPTER 26
Vegan Gold Digger

IVY

"You look good," says Christopher, looking me up and down with raised eyebrows.

"I doubt that very much," I reply. I'm wearing torn jeans and yesterday's shirt, my hair is in a messy bun, and I haven't seen a tube of mascara for days. Also, why is Christopher being nice all of a sudden? I eye him suspiciously. "What do you want from me?"

He barks a laugh and musses his hair. "I just mean ... with Alex. You look good with a baby. It suits you."

"Ah," I say. "I'm barefoot in the kitchen with a baby on my hip. You're into trad wives. Is that it?"

He laughs again. "No. I don't think so, anyway. Never met one."

"Nor has anyone," I reply. "They only exist on Insta."

"That's probably true. Either way, you should learn to take a compliment."

My jaw drops open. "I can take a compliment."

He gives me an uncertain look.

"I can!" I insist. "I'm just not used to them coming from *you.*"

"Why? Because I called you a vegan gold digger?"

"You *what?*" I demand.

Christopher bursts out laughing. "Only kidding, dude."

Baby Alex seems to think the conversation is fun and joins in with Chris's raucous laughter.

I wait for them to stop being childish—or, at least, for Christopher to stop being childish—then give him a pointed look. "I'm not vegan."

He roars with laughter again. I hand him the baby, put a bottle on to warm, and make myself a strong cup of coffee.

"Er," he says, holding Alex as if the baby is radioactive. "This is probably not a good idea."

"Can't hear you," I reply, leaning into the loud whirring of the fancy coffee machine.

There is mild panic in his eyes. "I don't want to drop him."

"So then don't drop him," I reply.

"Where's Mildew?"

"Brumilde is getting some well-deserved rest. If you wake her ... you'll be sorry."

"Why?" he grins. "What will you do? Put a hex on me?"

"Something like that."

"I don't doubt it," he continues, narrowing his eyes. "You do have, like, *witch* energy or something."

I smile back brightly. "As I said. You'll be sorry."

Blessed coffee in hand, I sit opposite them as Christopher awkwardly handles a squirming Alex.

"Good for you guys to bond," I say, enjoying Chris's discomfort. "If you play a game with him, he'll probably stop trying to escape from your clutches."

He looks at me as if I'm mad. A game that would be suitable for an infant? The only games he knows probably involve beer pong, or a poker hand and stripping.

"Peek-a-boo?" I suggest. I'm pretending to be an expert in this field, but it's the only baby game I know.

Before Chris can start hiding behind his hands, the front door opens and Henderson rushes in without greeting.

He practically yells at us. "News!"

I spring up, almost sloshing my coffee on the—very expensive, superbly impractical—carpet.

I can see it's good news by the extra twinkle in Henderson's eyes. His cheeks are flushed, making a welcome change from how pale he's been looking since Alistair disappeared.

Alex, startled by this development—and probably feeling unsafe in his uncle's vodka-scented embrace, starts whimpering.

"Mother!" Christopher yells in the general direction of the main suite. "Mother!"

Alex starts wailing, probably wondering why the big man is shouting. I take him, and his body relaxes immediately in my arms.

"I'd be nervous on Christopher's lap, too," I whisper to him. I shush him and kiss the top of his head, relishing the smell of his soft, clean hair.

I look expectantly at Henderson, but we wait till Isobel arrives.

"It's good news," I say to the bodyguard. I know it is. I can feel it.

He nods.

"Have you found him?" The question is out before I think it through. No, they haven't found him. If they had, Henderson would be with him, not walking into a penthouse saying something as infuriatingly oblique as "News".

But it's still good news. That's all that matters right now. I get Alex's bottle from the warmer and feed him while I wait the torturous three minutes for Isobel to arrive.

"And?" she demands, eyes alive with hope.

"Right," says Henderson. "I've got good news, and I've got even better news."

We all stare at him in absolute silence as if our lives depend on the words that come next.

"The severed ear was not Alistair's."

"Oh thank god," says Isobel, hand on her chest.

"It seems like it was just a trick to get our attention."

Christopher rubs his face. "Absolute *fuckers.*"

Isobel smacks his shoulder and gestures at the baby. If Chris feels chastened, he doesn't show it.

I'm too nervous to be relieved. "The better news?" I ask, my voice sounding gruff with anxiety.

Henderson smiles with a tight jaw; I can see that he's just as on edge as I am. He clears his throat. "Brodie got a match to the partial print on the gift box. We knew it belonged to a local biker. Our guys found him and extracted the details of the sender."

Ouch, I think. I hope the poor guy gave it up for a couple of thousand baht and wasn't subjected to any kind of ... *extraction* process.

"But we already *know* the details of the sender," says Christopher. "It's the Russian fuckers."

Alex chuckles at Isobel's grimace.

"We got the address," says Henderson, not able to keep the hope from his eyes. "*We got the address.*"

"Where they're keeping Alistair?" asks Isobel.

"My guess is yes."

"Then why are you here?" demands Christopher, a vein at his temple visibly throbbing.

Henderson puts out his hand. "I know, Chris, I know. It was my first instinct, too. But Brodie had already arranged a special ops force, a local team that know this area like the back of their hands. They have eyes everywhere, they speak the language, they know the dangers, and the secret doors and tunnels. Brodie promises it will be a slick operation, with less risk to Alistair than if we were to go in."

Christopher huffs, but it makes sense.

"They're already on their way," adds Henderson, taking his phone out of his jacket pocket and placing it on the coffee table. "We should have news soon."

I realize suddenly that I'm battling to breathe. I'm hot, sweating, and the colors in the room feel too bright. I can't get enough air.

"Ivy," says Isobel. Her voice cuts through the room like glass. "Are you all right?"

I nod, still trying to get oxygen, but my lungs are stuttering. She sweeps up to me and takes Alex, then orders Chris to get me a cup of tea. She takes my clammy hand in her confident one.

"It's going to be okay," she says.

I nod, but I can't talk. I have no words, anyway.

My gasping slows down, and slowly I get some air again.

She's gentle with me. "It's a lot to deal with, but Alistair is going to be fine."

How can she be so sure? We know nothing about this Thai special ops team. We know very little about Brodie. And what we do know about the Mirror Bratva is enough to give us all nightmares for life. There is absolutely no guarantee that Alistair is going to survive.

I realize I've been stuffing my feelings down because they're too scary to process properly. Making coffee, holding Alex, talking to Becks last night, acting like I was okay. Doing what I could to keep the looming shadow of death at bay. Trying to function like a regular human when my whole body is in a state of shock and grief because of the danger Alistair is in. How can I breathe when Alistair may never breathe again?

Christopher bangs a cup of strong tea on the table. "Don't say I never do anything for you."

I know he's trying to keep it light, but my body is glowing with anxiety.

Henderson's phone starts ringing. He looks down at the screen and exhales through pursed lips, then nods at us and answers the call.

CHAPTER 27

Blood Spatter

IVY

We all freeze.

Henderson answers the call on speakerphone. "Got him?"

Please god please god please god, I think. Any god will do.

"He wasn't there," says the strained voice. Brodie.

I let out an involuntary sob. My hopes had been so high that this nightmare was over.

Henderson looks like he's about to smash the phone, but catches himself just in time. He swallows audibly and flexes his fingers. "What happened?"

Don't freak the fuck out, I hear Becks say in my head. *They said he* wasn't *there. That's better than finding a dead body. If you panic now, you won't be able to think clearly. Just … breathe.*

We stare at the phone.

"Was it the wrong place?" asks Henderson. "Bad intel?"

Or worse, a trap?

"No. It was definitely the right place. Mr Ravenscroft's DNA was everywhere."

My stomach is a fist. *Everywhere?*

I look around wildly for someone to say something. Anything.

Henderson's trembling. "Blood?"

There's a pause. "Yes, but most of it wasn't his."

"*Most* of it?" demands Christopher. "What the fuck? What happened there?"

"Hard to tell from initial findings," replies the intern. "Definitely a struggle. A lot of cleaned-up blood spatter picked up with Luminol and UV. A body was removed, possibly two, judging by the smear pattern."

"But not Alistair's body," says Henderson.

"There's nothing to suggest that it was Alistair's body."

"And you're sure your special ops squad isn't playing both sides?"

"I'm sure. They want the Russians gone as much as we do. Having any kind of foreign criminal activity on their turf makes them nervous. It leaves them open to investigation when things go wrong."

"He's escaped," I whisper.

Isobel looks at me. "What was that, dear?"

"He's escaped. If it's true what Brodie says."

"Not necessarily," replies Christopher, but I can tell he's feeling more positive, too.

"You said so," I tell Isobel. "You said he's a survivor."

She nods. "We can only hope."

"There is a chance he got away," says Brodie, reminding me we were still on a call. "But we must prepare ourselves either way. Anything could have happened."

I remember Brodie following Blackwood into the Glass Baron's fake funeral, only to find his mentor's fresh corpse. Yes, we shouldn't get ahead of ourselves with these devious people. There is no knowing what really happened in that blood-spattered room.

But, deep down, I know that Alistair is alive. And I must get to him.

I spring up, then regret it, because I'm hit with a wave of dizziness.

Blood spatter. Smear pattern. Fresh corpse.

I feel hot and cold at the same time. Henderson is beside me, his strong hand steadying me. Once the floaty feeling passes, I nod at him. He returns the nod and lets go.

Isobel is concerned. "Ivy, dear. You're as pale as a sheet. Sit down."

"I need to go to him," I say, mouth dry with nerves.

Three pairs of wide eyes survey me, then they all talk at once.

Henderson's expression is stern. "No way is that happening."

I don't hear Isobel over Christopher, who splutters: "Jesus. The vegan's gone batshit crazy."

I want to tell him to fuck off, but if he didn't care about me, he wouldn't have said anything, so I'll take it as a win— except that he goes on. "Not enough steak in your life," he says, "makes you delulu."

Now I *do* want to tell him where to shove it, but I have more important things to do. I look around for my handbag and phone, then remember I have neither.

"I need money and a phone," I say to Henderson.

"Luckily for you, I have both of those things," he replies.

"You're coming with me?"

He scoffs. "As if I'd let you go alone."

She's a slow learner, this one, I can imagine him thinking.

"Good. Great. Thank you."

"I'm not sure about this," says Isobel, biting her perfectly made-up bottom lip.

I don't need her permission, but I do want to put her at ease. "I understand your concern. But if I'm right, and Alistair has escaped, he'll have no way to contact us. He'll try to find me. He'll go to the villa. All I'm going to do is go there and wait for him."

"The villa's not safe," she replies.

"Henderson will make it safe," I reply.

Isobel hesitates, then gives me a reluctant nod. Christopher rolls his eyes but pulls me into a bear hug. It's awkward but comforting. I kiss baby Alex on the head and am rewarded with a happy gurgle. I find that I don't want to leave him behind.

"So," says Henderson on the way down. "I bought you a new phone."

He takes it out of his pocket. The screen flashes under the elevator lights. Poor Henderson. This is, like, the fifth phone he's had to get me. It seems to be turning into a rather boring but expensive hobby.

"But here's the deal," he says. "You can't tell Rebecca Bradley where we're going."

I reach for the phone, but he doesn't let me have it.

"Becks is my best friend," I argue. "She's flown all this way to help me."

"Chat to her all you like," he says. "Just don't tell her where we are, or mention anything about the case."

I flush with frustration. "What else is there to talk about? It's the whole reason she's here! She understands the jeopardy."

Henderson's lips are a straight line. "If she understood anything, she wouldn't have brought an unvetted random into the picture."

"Noah isn't random. They've been dating for as long as Alistair and I have."

Henderson clears his throat and blinks at me. "Exactly."

Okay, fine. He has a point.

"And of course she's vetted him. She vets everyone. She's a thorough and talented investigative journalist."

"I'll brief Brodie on it when he's less preoccupied," says Henderson. "But, for now, you must promise me. Noah is to be regarded as dangerous until proven otherwise."

His eyes, usually twinkling and friendly, have an intense look to them now.

"Of course," I say, and I mean it. As irritating as I find Noah, I doubt he'd hurt a fly.

On the busy road outside the hotel, Henderson secures us a tuk-tuk.

"Seriously?" I say, climbing in. Never in a million years would I imagine smart-suited Henderson in a blinged-up tuk-tuk. It's all silver tassels, sequins, and stickers.

"It'll be quicker," he replies, and pushes cash into the driver's hand, saying something in Thai that I don't understand.

As the tuk-tuk navigates the bustling streets, my senses are bombarded with vibrant sights and sounds. Rows of colorful vendor stalls offer tropical fruits and freshly grilled spicy satays. Motorbikes weave expertly through the traffic, their riders balancing everything from live chickens and stacks of laundry to gas canisters and family members. In the distance, I see the top of the ornate spires of a gilded Buddhist temple. I take a breath and look at Henderson. I'm nervous as hell, but I have a mounting hope that this is finally going to be okay. Alistair is on his way home. I know it.

CHAPTER 28
Finish Line

ALISTAIR

Being out in the open air is crazy. I'm so used to being in the quiet, dark basement that being free is an assault on my senses. My eyes ache at the brightness of the sun, the constant honking and humming of the traffic makes my swollen brain throb. Street food vendors offer me food that makes me taste bile. I'm too hungry to eat. I guess there's a first time for everything.

I flag down a taxi and explain to the driver that I can only pay him at the destination. He doesn't seem at all concerned, and cheerfully ushers me into his car. I explain that I'll have to get out of the cab to get the money, and it may take a while. He just smiles and gives me a thumbs-up. I can't imagine this happening in London.

Sitting in the back seat, I'm again weighed down by everything that has happened, but then I allow myself the hope of seeing Ivy, and I begin feeling lighter. Could it really be possible that she'd be in my arms within hours? I dare to hope. Hope has been the thing that has kept me alive, kept me strong. I can get through anything if Ivy's at the finish line.

I start feeling euphoric. I close my eyes and think of her, and of Alex. Brumilde in her flour-dusted apron. My little cobbled-together family. I realize that I want to make things official as soon as possible. I'll get Henderson to begin the adoption process. Of course, this wouldn't technically be a legal adoption, but we'd be able to get the necessary paper-work to make it look official. Alex will be my son.

No. That's not right. What I mean is that *if* Ivy agrees, Alex will be *our* son.

But how can I ask Ivy to adopt a baby? It hardly seems fair to ask her to commit to a lifetime of parenting the child of strangers. She doesn't live under the constant shadow of the Mariya-shaped guilt that made me bring Alexander home to England.

She doesn't know the bad things I've done. She doesn't need the redemption I crave.

I look down at my newly acquired handgun.

Leaning forward, ignoring the shooting pain in my ribcage, I get the driver's attention. "Is there a ... a pawn shop nearby?"

CHAPTER 29
A Paper Bag

IVY

Henderson and I sit in uneasy silence at the villa. It's not so much awkward as nerve-wracking; we're both on edge and don't know what to do with ourselves. Would Alistair really come here if he had managed to escape?

I still have those awful words in my head: *blood spatter; fresh corpse,* and the hard-to-forget visual of a dismembered ear in a bloody gift box.

"Have you used your new phone yet?" Henderson asks.

I know what he's really asking. "I haven't told Becks what's happened or where we are."

"Good," he replies.

"Do you really think Noah is sus? He comes across as completely harmless."

Henderson clears his throat. "Everyone is suspicious until proven otherwise."

"He seems nice," I say. "He brought Becks all the way over here to see me."

Henderson doesn't look convinced. "Hmm."

Honestly, I feel the same way about Becks's new boyfriend. Why had I never heard of him? Why was he already springing for airfare so early in the relationship? Okay, fine, I was in no place to judge. I literally moved in with Alistair within days of meeting him. But ... still.

"I don't trust him, either," I admit. "But I never trust Becks's boyfriends. I think it's got more to do with me being possessive than anything else. Also, I wasn't in a great place when I met Noah. Everything was up in the air."

That was putting it mildly. I had barely survived The Great Swim and then, suddenly, there was a strange man in the hospital, saying he was with Becks. And she had that dreamy expression in her eyes. It worried me because it was out of character. Becks doesn't fall in love. Becks doesn't even get infatuated. She seems altogether too clever for that.

"She's got a good radar, though," I say. "Becks. She's a good judge of character."

Henderson makes a face.

"She just *pretends* she doesn't like you," I insist. "I see the gleam in her eye when you're in the room."

Henderson flushes and clears his throat. Oh my god! Why is he blushing? Is their enemies-to-lovers crush mutual? No way!

Also ... no wonder Henderson doesn't like Noah! Is this why I'm not sure about him? Poor Noah. He's probably just an innocent being caught in this cupid's arrow crossfire. Probably a really decent guy who has arrived at the wrong place at the wrong time.

Henderson is looking distinctly uncomfortable, so I change the subject. "Do you think Alistair will come here, to the villa? It all seems a bit too easy. Escape from the Russian mafia and head straight back to your holiday accommodation for a piña colada."

"Well, when you put it like that..." he says, a hint of a smile on his face. "Doesn't seem likely, does it?"

My expression must convey my dismay, because he quickly follows up.

"He'll come here. Where else would he go? He's no phone, no money, and no contacts in Koh Samui. This is the only address he knows."

I nod. Most people would go to the police, but I'm guessing he'll likely skip that part.

"Lucky has contacted all the hospitals on the island. They'll call immediately if someone who matches Alistair's description is brought in."

"That's not going to happen," says a gravelly voice from the front door.

My heart recognizes the voice and almost explodes in my chest. Everything is in slow motion as I turn my head to face Alistair, mouth open, eyes already filled with tears. His eyes are sunken, he has the beginnings of a beard, he's lost weight, his cheekbone is swollen, but he's alive.

Alistair is alive. The knowledge melts me.

Henderson jumps up. "Sir!"

If I stand I think I'll faint, but I do so anyway. "Alistair!" I sob.

"I'll call a doctor," says Henderson.

Alistair shakes his head, lifting his hand. "Not necessary."

"With all due respect," says Henderson, "I think it's very much so."

"It's nothing a shower and a whisky won't take care of."

My gaping mouth is yet to utter a word other than his name. "Alistair," I echo, willing myself to believe it; to believe that the nightmare is over. That the missing piece of my heart is back. I don't remember crossing the room, but the next thing I know is that I'm in his warm, strong arms, and I'm weeping like an inconsolable child.

"You're alive," I sob. "You're alive."

"Only because of you," he murmurs into my hair. He holds me tight, and I never want him to let go. We stand like that for a while, and then Alistair remembers something.

"Ah. Henderson. There's a cab driver outside—"

"Say no more," replies Henderson, grabbing his phone and wallet to go and pay the man.

"Give him a—" says Alistair.

"A huge tip, yes sir."

Alistair's grimy shirt is wet with my tears. He rubs my back gently, letting me cry, even though I should be the one holding him after what he's been through.

I look up at him. I'm still ugly crying. "Are you *okay?*"

He smiles. "I am. I'm fine."

"Are you hurt?"

He gives a little sigh. "Not much. A fractured rib or two, so now we match."

I think of Adam and Eve, but the analogy doesn't work.

"Your face," I say, wanting to touch it, but not wanting to hurt him.

"It's nothing," he says. "Just gives me a bit more character. Can you still love me when I'm this ugly?"

I laugh through the tears. You could put Alistair in a boxing ring with Muhammad Ali and he'd still be the most gorgeous man in the room.

I shrug. "I guess I could put a paper bag over your head."

He laughs and pulls me into his arms again. "God. I missed you. I thought about you constantly."

"Same," I say.

Alistair stops laughing, and his voice seems strained. "You got me through the worst of it."

We hug until Henderson comes back.

"Cab driver sorted, sir," he says, blinking rapidly. "May I have your permission to call your family and let them know you're back? Are you up for a debrief? I still want to call a doctor."

Alistair smiles again. "I appreciate your concern, Henderson. I'm fine."

"I'll get painkillers and antibiotics delivered ASAP. And food."

"And champagne," says Alistair, looking into my eyes. "We've never had more to celebrate."

I can't even think about food or booze. My whole being is vibrating with post-traumatic anxiety, and I'm not even the one who was abducted.

"Please do tell my family that I'm fine. And arrange a party. A feast, with no expense spared. Maybe on the beach."

"Today?" asks Henderson. "Tonight?"

"No," Alistair shakes his head. "Tomorrow." His eyes laser into mine. "Lock this place down. I need a completely uninterrupted twenty-four hours."

I blush.

"Yes, sir. Of course."

CHAPTER 30
Soap & Whisky

ALISTAIR

Seeing Ivy's beautiful face is the only painkiller I need. Her mere presence absorbs my aches and restores my strength. I did think I'd need medical care, but as soon as I saw her I felt healed. Mostly, anyway. Now and then there's a shooting pain through my torso, but it's nothing I can't deal with.

"I brought you a gift," I tell her.

Ivy closes her eyes and gives a quick chuff of a laugh. "Only you."

"What?"

"Only you would come back with a gift after being imprisoned by the fucking Bratva." Her smile fades. "Oh, god, it's not someone's head or something, is it?"

It's my turn to laugh. "No, darling. It's not. I had to leave that in the cab. The driver insisted."

She smacks my arm, then winces and apologizes.

"It's okay," I say. "I'm not fragile."

"Show me," she replies, her hand moving to my ass, and then to my cock. "Is this my gift?"

"It's not what I was referring to, but you're welcome to it."

"Do you know," she murmurs, "Do you know how many times I've fantasized about you since you've been gone?"

"Fewer times than I," I reply. "You were my constant companion in there."

"What was it like? The place they kept you?"

"Grim. And there was never enough water."

"Let me get you some!"

"I had plenty on the drive. Smashed two liters on the way here."

"I want to know everything," she says. "I want to help you heal."

"You're all I need to heal. I'm so relieved that you're okay. I'm so sorry I pushed you off the yacht. It must have been terrifying."

"Not as terrifying as seeing someone shoot you."

"I hated knowing you were down there in the cold dark water. I'll never forgive myself."

"You saved my life."

I feel a spark of anger. "Your life should never have been in jeopardy in the first place. You're my responsibility. It's my job to keep you safe."

"You did," Ivy insists.

"This will never happen again," I promise. "We're going to clean up the Ravenscroft operation for good, and we are never going to have to worry about this kind of thing again."

"I'd like to believe that. I don't think I can survive a repeat."

"You won't have to. This is the wake-up call the whole family needed. They'll be less reticent to halt illegal operations now. They'll see that it's just not worth it."

She nods, blinking away tears. She's honestly even more beautiful than I remember.

"When we lost Ariana to the Redbricks and father went off-kilter, there didn't seem a lot to live for. There was no one left to protect. It was easy to just focus on building the corporation, growing the bottom line without much thought of the consequences. But then ... you walked into my life."

Ivy gives me a cheeky smile. *"Fell* into your life."

I smile. "Now dangerous maneuvers no longer make sense. There's no amount of money in the world I wouldn't give up to keep you safe. I don't need to chase risks to feel alive."

"And now Ariana's back," she says. "Your father's doing better. And we have baby Alex."

Does she think of Alex as family? I wonder. Or if she doesn't, would she be able to?

"Exactly," I say. "It's time to clean up the shop and protect what really counts."

A wave of fatigue hits me like a brick wall.

Ivy notices. "You must be exhausted," she says. "Do you want to sit down? Or sleep?"

"No way I'm going to sleep now that I have you back," I reply.

She mock-scolds me. "You need to rest."

"What I really need is you. But, first, I'll shower."

"I'll listen out for the delivery," she says. "I'll cook something."

"Don't you dare." My voice sounds gruff. "Save all your energy for me."

Ivy, still tearful, chuckles. I haven't heard that in a long time, and it makes me think that everything is going to be okay.

I'll make it okay. But first: soap and whisky.

I use the outside shower. I don't like the idea of going into a closed room, and much prefer the open air and sunshine. When I reach to lather my shoulders, Ivy appears behind me and takes the soapy loofah from my hand. Slowly, gently, she washes my back in slow circles, then moves on to my arms, my legs, my torso. Grit and dried blood flake off and swirl around and down the plughole. Half my body is covered in bruising, and she takes extra care around any lacerations. She starts crying again when she sees the damage done by the rubber bullets, so I hang the loofah up and hug her, wetting her in the process.

"Good thing you're wearing a white T-shirt," I tease.

She looks down and laughs. The wet fabric is clinging to her breasts in the best way.

"You're the worst," she says, sniffing.

"Hmm-hmm." I pull her back towards me. I never want to let her go.

CHAPTER 31
Eat First

IVY

I can't believe Alistair is back. I'm still in shock. The good kind, of course, but my body doesn't seem to know that. I'm a mess of tangled nerves and shaking hands, and the tears keep coming, even when I'm sure I have none left. I can't get comfortable in my skin.

Fully dressed, I join him in the shower, and that makes me feel slightly better. The pounding of the warm water and the feeling of his skin seem to settle me a little. Once I feel a little better I step out onto the patio, peel off my wet clothes, and rub myself dry.

There is a rapping on the door. The knocking sequence tells me it's a bodyguard. I slip on the expensive-looking villa dressing gown and go to answer, first looking through the peephole, as I've been taught. I recognize the guy and open up. He greets me by name and brings in five heavy shopping bags, and then a case of champagne. He offers to unpack, but I'd prefer to do it.

I thank him and load up the fridge and the giant fruit bowl. There are plenty of cheeses and cured meats, so I think I'll arrange a charcuterie platter for us, like the one Brumilde put together on my first evening at the manor. I didn't feel hungry before, but I think eating will help get rid of this awful anxiety eating away at my stomach. And booze — I want it now. Anything that will help calm me down. I'm so highly strung that I wouldn't turn down Rohypnol if it were on offer.

You'd think that I'd be all happiness and rainbows now that Alistair's home safely, but my body feels like it's on fire inside, and not in a good way. I'm assuming it's the PTSD from my own kidnapping that is rearing up in my subconscious. I had worked with Dr Sandringham on releasing the trauma, and I thought it was going well. But these things take time.

I take a few deep breaths while I plate up the various treats. He probably won't want anything too rich, so this way he can pick and choose from the assortment on the board. Artichokes, olives, caper-berries, cured meats, spiced mango chutney with melting camembert and crumbly cheddar. Cheese straws and salty crackers. I add sliced apples and peach, and a bunch of grapes, along with some perfectly ripe figs. I skip the caviar.

I assume the champagne will be room temperature, but when I open the box, the bottles are cold, which I find very satisfying, and also a bit troubling, because I no longer recognize myself. I push down the discomfort and focus on the present moment. Alistair is all the matters right now.

The medication and dressing supplies are in the third bag, dessert in the fourth.

I find ice-cream, strawberries, freshly whipped cream, and a honey-ginger pot that I warm up in the fancy microwave. Maybe the sweetness will remind Alistair of better times. I put it all on a platter, too, so that we have one savory and one sweet.

When Alistair finds me in the lounge, he looks at the food and then back at me.

"So delicious," he growls. "I don't know who to eat first."

I chuckle and let my gown fall open just enough. "Now, I know what you're thinking."

"Do you?" he asks, an amused expression on his ridiculously good-looking face.

"You're thinking that you shouldn't be drinking champagne when you're wounded."

His eyes sparkle, making me think that he remembered this conversation from the first night we spent together. "That was not what I was thinking."

"So, in order to ... *mitigate the risk* ... I have water in the ice bucket for you, too."

He moves closer, his eyes hungry. "I appreciate your assuagement strategy."

"Now you're using billionaire words that I don't understand. You forget that I am an ordinary peasant."

Alistair kneels in front of me. "There is nothing ordinary about you, Ivy Mickelson."

Every single thing about me is ordinary. I don't know why Alistair thinks otherwise, but I can see he believes what he's saying, so I don't argue. If anyone in the room is larger than life and wonderful, it's him. Despite being a billionaire.

"You remember our first night together," I say.

"Every moment of it. You were suspicious of me, as you should have been."

"You carried me when I was unconscious. Bought me silk pajamas. Drew me a bubble bath."

"Red flags galore," he teases.

"You poured me my first glass of real champagne, which I promptly choked on."

"It was all planned. I was standing by to give you mouth-to-mouth."

I laugh. "Feels like years ago."

"Well," Alistair says, dragging his fingers down my naked thighs. "A lot has happened since then."

"Too much," I reply. "I hope things settle now. I'd like to have some peaceful time with you so that we can just relax and enjoy each other."

"Indeed," murmurs Alistair, his touch getting harder. "We haven't made nearly enough progress on our kink list."

"I bet you that if we had a few days and only that list to focus on, we'd be able to put a proper dent in it."

"Hmm," says Alistair. "I like that idea." He punctuates his sentence by reaching round to the small of my back and pulling my hips towards him, making me slide down on the couch, then passes me a chilled flute. He takes a sip of his, then begins licking my pussy, sucking my clit, slowly twirling it in circles with his magical tongue.

I close my eyes and relax into the pleasure. I can't believe he's back.

After a few minutes, he takes a break and has another leisurely sip, then looks me in the eyes. "God, I dreamed about this. I could do this all day long."

CHAPTER 32
You're My Kink

ALISTAIR

I dive back into Ivy's pussy. Fuck, I've missed her. Her cunt is everything. I go really slowly, savoring it, luxuriating in it, while I listen to her breathe and moan in pleasure. When I take my next break, she looks like a pile of jelly. The champagne is cold and dry in my mouth, the perfect contrast to Ivy's warm wetness.

She sighs long and hard. "I've missed you."

"You've missed *me?*" I tease. "Or my mouth?"

"The whole package, Alistair. The whole damn package."

"Shall I continue? Or would you prefer something else?"

"So polite! Where's that dirty mouth I know and love?"

"Oh, it's coming," I assure her. "I'm just getting warmed up."

"I want what you want," Ivy says, popping a grape into her mouth as if she's at brunch with friends instead of naked and spread-eagled before me.

"You can't keep saying that."

"But it's true. I get turned on when *you're* turned on. I've told you before. You're my kink."

"We're going to have to work on that," I tell her. "We'll have to do some more exploratory work."

"Where do I sign up?"

"You signed up when you agreed to be my pet."

"Best decision I've ever made," Ivy replies. "Just saying."

"Best offer I've ever made," I say, and we chink glasses.

"So what are you in the mood for?" asks Ivy. "Are you in pain?"

"There's no pain when you're in the room," I reply.

"I thought you might want it ... rough, like that time after Ariana's medevac. In that random hospital room."

My cock twitches. "I do. But first I want it sweet and slow. I want to taste every part of you. I want to fuck every part of you."

Ivy's lips part, her cheeks flush. "There's that filthy mouth that I know and love."

"This filthy mouth isn't done with you yet," I say, and go down on her again.

Ivy's swollen and juicy now. She throws her head back as I push my tongue into her as far as it will go.

She bucks her hips. "Fuck!"

I go back to sucking her clit while I push my fingers into her, knowing she can already take two because she's so wet. She moans as her muscles clench me. All the blood in my body flows directly to my cock, giving me a raging erection.

I'm relieved because nothing had happened when Ivy had joined me in the shower. It's extremely unusual for me to not have a hard-on when being soaped down by a beautiful woman, especially if that woman is Ivy. I had briefly wondered if the past few days had affected me more than I know, but I can push that out of my mind now. Ivy's ripe and ready, and my cock is acting like a heat-seeking missile.

I don't want to rush this. I want to fuck Ivy for hours, so I slow things down. I make little bites for her to eat—danish feta on a pesto cracker, a prosciutto rose, a fat olive stuffed with rosemary and pimento. I feed myself, too. We drink our champagne as I trace her body with my fingers, my hands, my lips.

"I didn't have 'naked sex picnic' on my bingo card for today," she jokes.

"Nor did I," I say. "But it's rather enjoyable. We'll do it more often."

Ivy runs her hands over my sore muscles, goes gently over the cuts and bruises, and kisses me softly, tasting of sharp cheddar and champagne.

When we've demolished the charcuterie, we take the champagne and dessert outside onto the patio and sit on a thick towel on the sun-warmed slats.

"Comfy?" I ask.

She nods and giggles uncertainly. She knows there is only one way to finish this feast.

"For old times' sake," I say, remembering the chocolate fondue. I check that the warm honey is the right temperature, and then I pour it over her breasts. She shrieks at the feeling and the mess. The ginger is aromatic.

"I remember this, too," she says. "A trip down memory lane."

"Are you saying I need to learn new tricks?" I ask.

Ivy shakes her head. "I'm pretty sure that you haven't shown me all of your original tricks."

"It'll be a sad day, indeed, once you've seen it all."

"I beg to differ," she replies, winking at me.

I should chuckle and continue the banter, but there's a sudden weird buzzing in my head. A vibration of sound and silver light that crowds my vision.

I see Anya.

"Whoah." I feel dizzy and put my hands on the deck to steady myself.

Ivy sits up. "Are you okay? You in pain?"

I blink at her. It's Ivy, of course. Anya's not here. Anya's dead.

"No. Just … a bit light-headed. Too much champagne," I fib.

"You're really pale," she says, eyes wide with worry.

"It's nothing," I say.

She looks for her robe to cover up. "We shouldn't be doing this. It's too soon. You should be in a hospital or something. I don't know what I was thinking."

"Nonsense," I say. "I'm fine. It was just a blip. A glitch in the matrix."

Ivy doesn't look convinced. "You need to see a doctor. Fly Syd over here if you have to. Or Sandringham."

I sigh. I know she's right but, honestly, it's the last thing I want to do.

"All I want," I whisper, "is to be with you and only you."

"Same," she replies, "but you need to be well for that to happen."

I can see by the obstinate look on her face that she's not going to budge.

"How about a lien," I say.

"Don't try to boggle me with your billionaire words again."

I laugh, and start to feel lighter again. I'm fine. I can deal with this. "Lien, from Latin, ligament, as in a bond. You give me something now on the promise that I will pay you back in the future."

"I give you sex now and you go for therapy when we're back home?"

"Exactly. And in the meantime, I get to keep you."

"Well," she says. "I like the sound of that."

"Good. Pleasure doing business with you, as always, Miss Mickelson. Shall we shake on it?"

"I'll go one better than a handshake," she says, and before I know it, my whole cock is in her mouth.

CHAPTER 33

Stormy Sex

IVY

Alistair's cock is always delicious. Now, smeared with honey, even more so. I work his shaft with both hands, slippery and sticky, while I swirl my tongue around the head and tease the hole with my tongue. I'm sure my face is a mess, but I don't care, pressing my face into his beautiful strong cock, sucking his balls, massaging his taint. He has all but collapsed on the patio, moaning and whispering "Feels. So. Good."

I've missed his body so much that I feel like I could swallow him whole. I try to keep everything slow, like he asked me to, but it's difficult. I'm burning up, needing him inside me.

Sweet and slow, he said. Just this time. Sweet and slow like shy lovers, like adoring couples. After what he had been through, no wonder he wants a gentle touch.

I push him all the way into my mouth, till I feel him touching the back of my throat, and I swallow his head over and over again as he moans, his hips moving in time.

Still holding him, I pull back, freeing my mouth to talk. "You wanna fuck my throat?" I whisper.

He nods. We swap positions so that I am lying on the towel again. He uses a sun lounger arm to steady himself as he lowers his thick cock into my open mouth. He goes slowly, gently opening me up, and it feels so good. I love the feeling of having him in my mouth. He goes further, easing his cock into my throat as I relax the muscles to avoid gagging.

Becks told me once that she thinks gagging while deep-throating is hot. I'm not a fan. Not yet, anyway, but who knows where our kink list will take us?

Alistair holds my cheek, checking to see if I'm okay. I nod and open wider. He soon finds a slow, gentle rhythm, and the look on his face makes me so horny. His body tenses and I think he's going to come, but he holds off. I'm relieved because I really need him inside me.

He withdraws, then levers me into a sitting position and sits beside me. Our naked bodies, sticky with honey, have made a mess of the towel. I grin at him, sure I look ridiculous with my messy face and swollen lips. Alistair moans and kisses me, gently biting my lip.

"I'm desperate," I murmur into his mouth. "I'm desperate for your cock."

I ignore his bruises. It makes it difficult to focus on pleasure when the reminders of his pain are so obvious. I say "his pain," but it's my pain, too.

"I've been dreaming of your perfect pussy for days," he replies. "I feel like this is too good to be true."

"It's true," I say, increasing my grip on his thigh to prove the point. Then I take his hands and move them over my breasts, my ribs, my stomach. "Can you feel that?"

Alistair nods.

"You can feel my warm skin? It's real. I'm here and I'm all yours."

"Yes," he replies, his voice gruff.

We kiss again, luxuriating in the knowledge that we are together again, safe and connected. We may be brutalized, traumatized, and exhausted, but we're together.

"I never want to leave you," I say.

"I should hope not," he replies. He's teasing me, but he knows what I'm saying because he pulls me in tighter.

"I can't stand the idea of you ever being in danger again. I can't handle it."

Alistair takes my cheek again. "You're fierce, Ivy, you can handle anything."

"No," I shake my head. "I can't. I was unraveling without you."

He looks sad, which makes me upset, and my eyes well up *again*. Honestly, I'm surprised I have any tears left.

"We're going to clean up the corporation," he says. "I've lost my appetite for risk."

"You've said that before," I remind him. It hadn't gone down well at the family lunch.

"I was committed then, and I'm more committed now."

"In your defense," I say, "after committing the first time, the Redbricks forced your hand. And then the Kuznetsovs—"

"Yes. We'll have to neutralize both threats if we are to have any kind of peace. It's not going to be easy, but it must be done."

It's a relief to hear this—to hear how serious he is about it, but I know it's not going to be close to impossible. How do you neutralize evil?

It's an abstract question for another time. Right now, I don't want to think about the Bratva, or the rival mafia family in Manchester. But I don't want slow and sweet lovemaking, either.

"Are you ready to get a bit ... rougher?" I ask.

I want it, but I think Alistair *needs* it.

Stormy sex is how he transforms his shadow energy into light, and I'm here for it.

CHAPTER 34

Craving You

ALISTAIR

Ivy's had enough of being sticky, so we head back into the shower and rinse the honey off. It's hot and humid, so we retreat into the perfectly air-conditioned bedroom with a fresh bottle of champagne. I wonder if it'll give me a closed-in claustrophobic feeling, but it doesn't. Not when Ivy's with me.

I light candles and warm some oil, and put on a bedroom playlist, which fills the room with heavy bass and breathy lyrics. The artist is being fucked in the luxurious changing room of a high-end store—a popular designer label—and the diamond crucifix on her necklace is bouncing on her chest rhythmically as her lover thrusts in. It's amazing what stories you hear if you listen.

"You okay with this?" Ivy asks.

I frown at her. What is not to like? A giant bed smothered in satin sheets, horny music, chilled champagne, and the promise of Ivy's pussy.

"I'm just wondering if it's too much," she says. "Stimulation overload. After what you've been through. Like, life after solitary detention. It can be overwhelming."

I chuckle. "No. It's perfect. It's everything I was craving while I was in there."

"You were craving dirty rap?"

I pull her toward me. "I was craving this body." I bury my head in her hair, and it's the exact fragrance I remember. "This head." My hands move down her body. "This perfect ass."

"My ass has been craving you," she teases.

My cock swells. "Well. Let's see what we can do about that." I push her onto the bed.

She giggles, surprised. Then her smile turns hungry. "Fuck, I'm horny. I want you so much."

Jesus Christ. This woman will be the death of me. She's too much, in the best way possible. I have to hold myself back. The savage inside me wants to just smash right into her and come immediately, especially after that epic deep-throating outside.

I breathe calmly through my nose, keeping it together.

"You feel stronger than before," Ivy says. "Tougher. Like a ... cage fighter or something."

If anything I had lost strength, but I guess the weight loss has made me look more cut.

"Wild and ripped," she continues. "Like you're ready to join fight club."

"I'm not sure if you're insulting me, or complimenting me," I drawl. "But I'll take it."

"Are you kidding?" she says. "Cage fighters are hot as fuck."

I'm pretty sure she's joking, but it's hard to tell when she has that horny expression.

"You're full of surprises," I say, edging nearer the bed.

"I like to keep you guessing," she replies. "Otherwise you'll think I'm just a boring granola bar and get tired of me."

I choke on my laugh. "Granola bar."

"With all due respect, Mister Ravenscroft. Why are we talking about fight club and granola when we could be ... *not* talking?"

"I'm just taking my time. Exercising patience. Otherwise, it'll all be over in seconds."

Ivy guffaws. "I'll believe that when I see it. Sex Marathon should be your middle name."

"Trust me, the way I'm feeling about you right now ... the way you look ... I don't stand a chance. I'll need to stare at the wall and think of my grammar school maths teacher."

"Don't you dare," warns Ivy.

When I don't move, she gets off the bed, so I have to throw her back onto it.

Her eyes are on fire. "That's more like it," she says.

Something deep inside me ignites. A little flame in my pelvis. I must have her.

"I want to go all the way," Ivy says.

My cock twitches again. "Don't we always?"

"More," she says. "Deeper. Harder. I want you to go as deep as you can in every way."

Fuck. My balls ache for her. I can't help touching them.

Her lips. So kissable. Ivy issues a challenge. "Go further than you ever have with anybody."

My breathing becomes heavy. I haven't touched her yet but I'm already on the edge.

I won't tell her this, but that won't be possible. She's not ready for my darkest self. I have lost myself in other women in ways that degraded them. She's too precious for that. I can't say that, so I pretend to agree. A while lie to protect us both. But she's not stupid—so I'll have to make her believe it.

"In that case," I say. "I'll need some equipment."

I go to the closet and find my bag of sex toys. I also reach for the crop and a barely-there black teddy with suspenders and tights. Ivy uses the time to drink her glass of champagne. She'll need the Dutch Courage.

I toss her the lingerie, and she lifts her brows in curiosity and approval. She puts them on while I warm some of the toys I plan on using. She looks at herself in the full-length mirror, narrowing her eyes as if there's something missing, then applies red lipstick. Perfect. It makes me want to put my cock in her mouth again, to see those ruby lips stretched around my girth. I let out a guttural moan and pull her into me. We're still in front of the mirror, and I'm stroking her curves with flat palms, kissing her stained lips until the makeup is smudged. I pull back and use my fingers to smear it more. A daub across her face; a mark of my territory. I kiss her deeply, roughly, forsaking elegance and technique for passion. Ivy's breathing quickens.

I draw my lips away, but I'm not finished with her mouth yet.

I put my thumb on her bottom lip, testing her, seeing if she wants more. Her lashes flutter, but she maintains eye contact. Ivy scoops up my thumb with her mouth and sucks it. Her tongue is warm and slippery. I demand more with my thumb, sticking it in deeper, and Ivy takes it. I feel her relax in my arms, opening up to me, wanting more. Her head tilts slightly back, wanting as much as I'll give her. I glance over our reflection as I add more. Four fingers explore her mouth and the exquisitely smooth skin of the inside of her mouth. I lower my face to her, kissing and licking her top lip as my hand goes further in.

Fuck. My cock is so hard.

She moans, sending a vibration through my fingers. I slowly remove them, smearing her lips one last time, then turn her to face the mirror while I stand behind her and reach for the crop.

CHAPTER 35
Black Leather Butterfly

IVY

Alistair has me stand in front of the full-length mirror. My lips are swollen, and my lipstick is a red smudge. The expensive barely-there teddy I'm wearing makes me look like a French courtesan, a *cocotte*, a high-end prostitute who knows her worth. I need winged kohl eyeliner, a cigarette, and a coupe glass of papillon to complete the picture. Not that I've ever actually tasted a papillon or met a French lady of the night—that's what books are for.

I love the version of me behind the glass. It's a sexy sophistication I've never tried to pull off before, luxurious and rich but with a slightly seedy undercurrent. The combination of the dim light and champagne is an excellent Insta-filter. I see no imperfections, only a seductive and sensual version of myself.

Alistair holds a black leather riding crop. He stands behind me and slowly strokes my back with it, sending shivers down my spine. Then, watching me in the mirror, he transfers the tingling touch to the front of my body, sweeping it delicately over my shoulders, collarbone, stomach, and breasts. My nipples swell under the impossibly light touch.

I want it to go on forever.

I want it to stop so that Alistair uses his full strength on me.

His left hand holds my jaw as we watch each other, breathing together, eyes liquid with desire as the small leather flap at the end of the shaft titillates every inch of my hungry skin.

Just as it becomes too much, he travels to the back of my body again. Alistair drags it from my ankle, all the way over the swell of my stockinged calf, the sensitive back of my knee, and lands where my thighs meet, causing a little explosion of desire laced with pleasure. He flutters it there for a while—a black leather butterfly between my legs. My pelvis starts to ache with the blood flow it's demanding, swelling my lips and clitoris.

Alistair strokes my butt, now. I watch his face, slack-jawed with carnal drive.

Jesus Christ, he's gorgeous. The strong line of his brow, the curve of his lips. The man is a god. It was my first thought when I met him, and it abides.

The crop flap circling the sensitive skin on my ass, I whisper, "You're so fucking hot."

He drags his gaze up to the mirror to look at my reflection, then moves the teddy strap off my shoulder and kisses the spot it had been touching. "I pale in comparison," he murmurs.

It's not true, but I let him get away with it because I am looking quite fucking hot, if I do say so myself. It's the candlelight, expensive lingerie, and the champagne filter, but I'll take it.

My clit is still humming, and I wonder how long it will take for Alistair to finally give me his cock. I have a restless feeling that he's in no rush at all.

The crop travels up to my face. I close my eyes and enjoy the sensation. When it nears my lips, I open my mouth, and it flutters on my lips and tongue, making my pussy pulse.

Then it's gone.

I gasp and my eyes fly open as I hear a snap and feel the sting on my ass. The pain is exquisite. I exhale a long stream of breath. Alistair lashes me and I gasp again. And again. I'm sure I have little pink marks under the sheer nylon. I put my hands on either side of the mirror to steady myself. He falls to his knees and rips open the thin fabric, pushing the teddy aside to examine the angry skin. He moans and kisses them, then licks them, sucking the flesh into his mouth so that I can feel his teeth.

"Perfect stockings, ruined," I say.

Alistair growls. "It's not the only thing I'm going to ruin today."

"Please," I say, voice wobbling. "Fuck me. I need you so badly."

He chuckles. "No, love. We're not even close. I'm going to spend hours worshipping this body."

My voice is guttural. "I can't wait that long."

"Unfortunately for you … you're not in charge."

CHAPTER 36
Delicious Pussy

ALISTAIR

I'm big talk about making Ivy wait for her orgasm, but the truth is that I'm dying to get inside her. We've never gone this long without sex, and my cock is making its frustrated desire known. My whole body aches to be clenched inside her delicious pussy. I reach around to kiss her, then walk her over to the bed.

"On your stomach," I growl.

She hesitates, so I push her onto the bed. I know she loves that. I follow it up by joining her on the mattress, keeping her down while I reach for the ropes.

I unlace her teddy. It's undamaged, but the stockings will have to be thrown away. I pull them off slowly—a snake shedding its skin. Ivy's pale body is glorious in its nakedness.

I've upgraded from the rope we used before—the tasseled ropes that hold the heavy velvet curtain back in my family home. My new purchase from my go-to sex shop looks similar—same-ish size, and golden—but this one is especially made for Shibari. Strong, but soft on the skin. I don't have the patience for Shibari today, but the velvet rope is handy for tying Ivy down. I knot it around her wrists and ankles and lash her to the bed. She's a starfish.

"You okay?" I ask, when Ivy's been quiet for a while.

"Yes," she replies. "Just enjoying the sensation."

This pleases me. I rub my cock. "I could look at you all day."

"Please don't," she replies. "I want your skin on mine."

I tie her hair up in a messy bun and drench her in the coconut oil I've warmed. She's moaning in pleasure before I even touch her, the decadent oil running down her sides and pooling in every crevice. I breathe in the moment, wanting to remember it forever. Twenty-four hours ago I didn't know if I'd live to see another day, and what a day it has turned out to be. Ivy could be dead—drowned in the ocean—and I could be bullet-riddled, dismembered, languishing in a Thai dumpster. But we fought and we survived. It makes this erotic encounter all the more heady.

I want to say something, want to acknowledge this, but I stop myself. Knowing we narrowly escaped death may be a turn-on for me, but it might send Ivy tumbling back into terrifying memories, so I keep quiet.

Instead, I communicate with my hands, rubbing the oil into Ivy's perfect skin, massaging every inch of her delectable body, from her delicate feet all the way up to the neck I love to kiss. She groans as I work my knuckles into her muscles. My thumbs seek every tense part of her and release the tension.

"God, you're good at this," she drawls. "If I died now, I'd die happy."

Hmm. Maybe she *had* been thinking of our fortunate survival. "Please don't die," I joke.

"It would be the ultimate cock-block," she agrees.

I chuckle. "So dark, Ivy."

I've massaged every bit of her except her best parts. I can't wait to get started on her ass.

"You mentioned earlier that your ass missed me?"

"Oh, it did," she replies.

"Okay," I say. "We'll have to do something about that."

I pour oil over her round cheeks. I see it dripping down the cleft and coating her labia.

Fuck.

Gritting my teeth for restraint, I start rubbing her ass, swirling my palms over the double-moon. She moans.

"You like that?" I ask.

"It feels so *good*," she groans.

I take my time, enjoying every minute. My cock is so erect it touches my abs as I work on Ivy.

Next, I lift Ivy's hips up and place a wedge pillow beneath her. The wedge angles her pelvis in such a way that exposes her velvety skin perfectly, making her easily accessible. I sink down between her legs—her magnificent spreadeagled legs—and start lapping at her clit with my tongue.

She lets out a long rolling moan. "Fuck. Alistair."

I'm nodding and licking, stopping only to suck her clit and squeeze her slippery ass. Her moaning gets louder. She's getting close.

I know not to change anything while she's ramping up like this. I keep my rhythm the same, steadily notching up her pleasure. I keep going until her breathing becomes ragged and her fingers are curled into fists.

Then I pull away.

"Don't stop!" Ivy sobs.

"I'll keep going," I promise her. "But you were getting too close."

She pretends to cry. "Please, Alistair."

"Not yet," I reply. It's important to me that this is the very best sex she's ever had in her life. It has to be *everything.* I'm going to edge her until she's choking for it. I want every nerve in her body to be ready, every body part charged with erotic energy. I'm going to turn her core into an explosive, and I'm the only one with access to the detonator.

I go back in for another session of licking her perfect pussy. She squirms. My balls ache as if they're in a vise.

"Please, Alistair," she begs, helplessly tied down by my golden rope. "Please fuck me. We can do whatever you want after. But now, please. I need your cock inside me."

"Soon," I say. "I haven't had enough of your body, yet."

I've been working on Ivy for around an hour but haven't yet had my fill. I'm not going to take this body for granted, not after what we've been through.

Ivy growls in frustration, pulling at the rope. I surprise her with one finger, and she gasps.

"Yes," she says, hungry for it, hungry for more.

Two fingers.

Ivy clenches them, and I start moving them in and out. So fucking warm and slippery.

"You're so wet," I tell her. "So tight."

I don't know how I fit into this pretty pink cunt, it's so small and delicate.

She squeezes me. Her pussy might look delicate, but her muscles are not. Thumb on her clit, I rub the pads of my two fingers against her G-spot. She inhales sharply and moans. I tap the spot for a while, then go back to stroking while she moans into her pillow.

"Ready for more?" I ask.

"Yes. Yes," she replies. "More."

I unzip my bag slowly, letting her hear it open all the way.

CHAPTER 37
A Filthy Kind of Heaven

IVY

Oh my god, I'm stuck somewhere between heaven and hell. No time for limbo, I bounce between the two. One minute I'm about to erupt like a volcano, the next I'm crying for Alistair because I'm frantic to have him inside me. Every time my orgasm nears, he does something to keep it at bay, and every time he does that, it comes back bigger. A snowball rolling downhill, picking up snow as it goes. Except that this is all fire, no ice. I'm actually nervous for when he decides it's time for me to come, because I don't know if I'll be able to handle it.

Fear, lust, desire, love, and adrenaline all pummel me with greasy fists. My insides are molten lava.

How will I get out of this alive? Will I get out of this alive? It doesn't feel likely.

I almost stop him. I almost say it's too much to handle, but then the waves of absolute pleasure wash over me and I know I want him to keep going. I want to experience everything he's willing to give me, even if it makes me scared.

I've lost count of the fingers inside me, but they're pressing against *everything* and it feels incredible. He's touching parts of me I never knew existed. It's so much, almost too much.

I gasp, and he eases off.

"Fuck," I murmur.

"I'm opening you up," Alistair says. "Opening you up so that I can fuck you with everything I have."

His gruff voice makes me want to come. I'm so turned on. So close to coming. My muscles start tensing.

"No, Ivy," he scolds. "You're not coming yet."

"Alistair!" I sob. "Please."

"Just a little longer."

I want to tell him that I don't know if I'll be able to handle the orgasm. It's too much. It's nothing like I've ever felt before. I don't know if it's the riding crop, the rope, the hour-long decadent massage, or his expert tongue and fingers, but my whole body is sparking with the inevitable orgasm and I can tell it's going to be *intense.*

I've certainly never been afraid of an orgasm before. But this—this is otherworldly. There is static in my head, as if the intense pleasure has short-circuited my brain. My body no longer belongs to me. I'm swimming in warmth, tingling all over.

He pushes his fingers in deeper, and I cry out. He is opening me, as he promised. Opening up my pussy, my body, my soul.

"Fuck!" I exclaim.

"Too much?" he asks.

"Almost," I whisper. "So intense."

I think he'll ease off, but he goes deeper still. I feel so filled up. My muscles threaten to spasm. I think they might be in shock, like I am. Surely he won't go further.

Famous last words, I hear an imaginary Becks say.

Alistair stretches me wide. I am a dahlia opening up to him; blooming and swelling and wet.

I'm starting to feel like I'll lose control of my body. It's simultaneously scary and inviting. An irrational impulse tells me that it's too much, that if I fall off this particular cliff, I will die.

Alistair reads my mind. "I've got you," he says, voice strong and deep.

I'm on the brink of tears. I nod. I know he's got me. I feel safer with Alistair than I have with anyone else in my whole life. He's the only person with whom I can truly let go.

Gradually, he removes his fingers, and instead of being relieved, I feel bereft and empty. I realize that I enjoyed being on the Orgasm Cliff of Death.

"Ready for more?" asks Alistair.

"More?" There couldn't possibly be more. "Yes, please," I say.

A warm, lubed dildo touches my entrance. It feels huge. My spine tingles with fear and longing. I breathe slowly, trying to relax my body.

"If it's too much, I'll stop," Alistair murmurs.

The tip of the dildo slides in and I groan as the pleasure radiates throughout my pelvis.

"Fuck," I whimper.

Alistair hums in pleasure. "So good," he whispers. "I love this pussy." Unhurriedly, he slides the rest of the huge shaft inside me, making my body weak. My moan grows louder with every inch. All my energy is in my pussy and there's nothing left for my limbs. My whole body *is* my pussy.

He starts moving the girthy dildo in and out, deliciously slowly, and it feels incredible.

I'm *definitely* going to come. No one will be able to stop the earthquake that's building in my body. Not me, not Alistair.

God almighty, if he/she exists, would not be able to stop this volcano from erupting.

Alistair makes a hissing noise, as if trying to contain his own pleasure.

Good luck with that, billionaire.

He works the dildo faster, and I can't stand the pleasure. No words come out, only gasping and ragged breaths. There's static in my brain again. Stars. Short-circuiting.

"Fu-u-u-uck," I whisper as the orgasm rolls toward me. It's a giant wave of warm water ready to smash into me. "Fu-u-u-u-ck!"

"This is so fucking hot," growls Alistair. "You're such a good girl. I love watching you take this."

I have no words.

"So fucking hot," he whispers again, increasing his pace, clearly wanting to kill me.

I'm going to explode all over him.

"You ready for your first orgasm?" he asks.

First orgasm. As if I'll survive it.

I nod. Or at least, I think I nod. I'm not sure I have any control over my body right now.

"Let me hear you say it."

Is he mad? Does he not realize that speaking is beyond my capability right now?

"R-ready," I whisper.

"Hmm?"

"Ready!" I gasp.

He waits.

Jesus Christ. Okay. "I'm ready for ... my first orgasm."

"Just one for now," he cautions. "I want to be inside you for the next one."

Dildo pushed to the hilt inside me, Alistair holds it against my G-spot with one hand while he finds my clit with the other. I'm going to come apart. I'm going to melt. This is everything.

But he still has more up his sleeve. He lowers his face to my pussy, licks around the base of the dildo, and then moves his warm tongue over my taint and starts circling my rim in wet lazy circles.

If there was a big red button to blow up the whole world, he's busy pressing it.

I pull on the golden ropes. My throat makes a weird gurgling sound. Probably a death-gurgle. My toes are over the cliff edge, and the earthquake is here. I feel sparks everywhere; I'm holding fireworks in my hands. There's a bomb rocking my pelvis, fuse lit, flame racing. I have mere seconds to live. There is a spicy tingle in my hands and feet as the sweeping pleasure leaves no square inch of skin untouched.

Wut. I can feel the orgasm in my hands and feet? *Oh, yes.*

"I'm coming," I whisper. "I'm coming."

He rubs my clit. He drags his tongue up and down, and back to my rim.

I'm scared because I have completely lost control.

I remember Alistair's words. *I've got you.*

Also: I'm opening you up so that I can fuck you with everything I have.

"It's time to let go," he says. "You're safe. I've got you. Come for me."

"Fuck, fuck, fuck!" There's nothing to do but surrender.

He pushes the tip of his tongue into me and I EXPLODE.

Full. Body. Orgasm. Detonation.

I'm flung into outer space, brain fizzing, golden sparks everywhere as if the golden rope has exploded along with my body. The volcano has erupts inside me.

Jesus Christ. I'm still flying. Muscles spasming, fireworks sparkling.

"I'm still coming," I cry.

The rope keeps me spreadeagled. How can I still be coming? Either this is the world's longest orgasm, or I have died and been sent to a filthy kind of heaven.

Alistair keeps going.

I may be in outer space, but he's still in between my splayed thighs, tonguing and rubbing and now fucking me with the giant dildo and I'm going to die again.

"FUCK!" I shout as the final climax crashes into me, shaking me, tossing me on its choppy surface.

FUCKING HELL. I have never.

I lose everything and I don't care.

My muscles push the dildo out. Alistair hisses a "Yes," because he knows what that means. I squirt all over him, all over the bed. It's such a release that I cry.

I'm ruined and I don't care.

I'm dead and I don't care.

CHAPTER 38
Grimy Fantasy

ALISTAIR

Jesus H. Christ.

I've seen a lot of women come in my life, but this was exceptional. Suffice to say I'm thoroughly soaked.

I'm elated. Ivy, on the other hand, seems unconscious.

"Ivy?" I touch her shoulder. "Ivy?"

When she doesn't answer, I untie the ropes and cradle her, kissing her forehead and stroking her arm. Her eyes flutter open.

"Are you okay?" I demand, amused but also slightly concerned.

"That's not the exact word I'd use," she murmurs.

"You're breathing," I say. "That's a good sign."

She chuckles weakly.

I caress the marks on her wrists. "I feel like I've just broken my favorite toy."

"You have," she replies. "I'm broken. Ruined forever."

"Were you ... unconscious?"

"Maybe. I think I was clinically dead for a moment. Everything went black. I disappeared."

I had heard of women blacking out when an orgasm was too intense, but I always thought it was an exaggeration. An urban legend. Poor Ivy.

I move a strand of her hair out of her face. "I feel I owe you an apology."

A stronger chuckle. "For giving me the longest, most intense, most amazing orgasm I've ever had in my life?"

"For almost killing you," I reply.

"Worth it," she says. "No apology necessary. Unless you'd like an apology from me, for basically fire-hosing you."

I laugh. "Worth it," I say, and kiss her.

I pour us each a glass of champagne and change the sheets. I'm still horny as fuck, but seeing as Ivy passed out and all, I'm giving her some time to recover. Her eyes are glazed over, her body limp.

"How much longer do we have?" she asks.

"What do you mean?"

"Time has become unstable," she says. "I was coming for days. How much longer do we have together before we have to show our faces? And look like regular humans?"

"You, Ivy Mickelson, will never look like a regular human."

She huffs. "You know what I mean. Till our big family lunch on the beach."

I look at my watch. "Eighteen hours?"

"Thank god. That's exactly how long I need to sleep. To recover."

I laugh. "Could we telescope that down to ten minutes recovery? It's about as long as I can wait."

Her chuckle sounds a little crazed. "Not unless you're into necrophilia."

"Wow. That went dark fast."

"So did my brain when you killed me."

"I'll be gentle," I say, cupping her cheek. "I'll bring you back to life."

"In that case," she drawls, stretching her long legs. "I'll be recovered as soon as I finish this." She tips the rest of the champagne into her mouth and swallows it. My gaze lingers at her throat.

"You've come a long way," I say.

She looks at me deadpan. "Ha ha."

"No, I mean from the first time we met."

"Do you mean when I choked on the champagne?"

I grin at her. "Now look at you. Downing a glass like the holy royalty you are."

"*Holy* royalty?" she puts her glass down. "I'm not sure I even know what that is, but I've clearly been upgraded."

I watch Ivy's beautiful naked body as she comes over to me on her knees. She cups her breasts as if she's presenting her body to me. I breathe deeply, my cock swelling as I watch her.

"Will you fuck holy royalty?"

"When you put it that way," I reply. "How could I resist?"

Not breaking eye contact, she touches her mound. "You opened me up. I'm so ready for you."

Jesus.

"I'm still tingling from that earth-shattering full-body orgasm. Having you inside me is going to feel so good."

"I'm going to make you come again."

Ivy laughs. "I doubt it. I think I'm all orgasmed out."

"We'll see about that," I growl.

I've always liked a challenge.

Ivy has a mischievous glint in her eye. I'm sure she's thinking something like *Are we really going to do this again? Sex marathon, anyone?*

My answer would be a resounding *yes*. After all that time without her, I'll take every minute with her that I can get.

Ivy gets closer. "Shouldn't we ... I don't know, rehydrate or something? Get supplies? Eat a protein bar?"

I chuckle. Although, to be honest, a protein bar would come in handy right now.

"We don't need supplies," I tell her. "I won't be long."

"Famous last words."

"Seriously," I murmur. "I'm so turned on, it's not going to take much."

I take her wrists in my hands and kiss the faint pink stripes left by the golden rope. "These marks will be interesting to explain to the family tomorrow."

Ivy laughs. "They won't even be looking at me. They'll be so glad to see you alive and well. You're cruel, not going to them right away. They were beside themselves with worry."

"You know what would be more cruel? Making someone who has just escaped confinement have to sit and drink tea with his family instead of eating out this glorious pussy."

"Well," she grins, eyes still sparkling. "When you put it that way."

I nuzzle her neck, and she sighs.

"As I was saying before ... I like this feral version of you," she says. "Don't get me wrong, I love the perfectly-groomed designer-suit version of you, too. It's super hot. But this is ... interesting."

"Feral?" I laugh. "Really?"

"You know what I mean. This dark version … the grimy version of you."

Rude. "I showered an hour ago!"

"I don't mean *actual* grime," she teases. "I mean dirty, like a dirty secret. Grimy fantasies."

"You are my ultimate grimy fantasy," I tell her.

"And you are my favorite feral lover," she replies.

"Your favorite? Do you have many? Feral lovers, I mean?"

"Oh, loads," she teases. "But none that compare to you."

I spank her and grab the rope again. "You're going to pay for that."

CHAPTER 39
Christmas Tree

I can't believe we're going to do this again. Alistair says it will be quick, but that will be a first. Still thirsty, my eyes land on the champagne.

"Do you remember that night?" I ask him. "With the champagne bottle?"

"Of course I do," he growls. "I'll remember it till my dying day. In fact, when my life passes before my eyes, I hope that's the scene that lasts."

I sigh. "All this talk of death and dying." I know I started it.

Alistair arranges my body on the bed. I'm on my back this time, knees bent, legs apart.

"Death is an aphrodisiac," he replies. "*Memento Mori*—it reminds you that life is short and it's time to make hay."

I snort. "Make hay? Is that what the youngsters are calling it nowadays?"

"You tell me," replies Alistair. "You're disgustingly young."

I make a shocked face. "Am *not*. I feel ancient."

"Wait till you get to my advanced age."

I laugh. "You certainly don't have the libido of a man of advanced age."

"That's because I have you."

"Your billionaire's pet," I say. "Where's my collar?"

"Ah," he replies. "You want a collar, do you?"

I had been kidding, but why not? I've never had one before. "I told you. I want anything you want to give me."

Alistair kisses my wrist, then inhales deeply at my neck. "God, you smell delicious. I want to give you everything."

He holds my jaw in his hand and searches my eyes. It's always a jolt when we look at each other like this, like there is electricity flowing between us.

"I love you so fucking much," he says. "I've never felt like this before."

I nod. "Same."

"I just knew when I met you."

My heart is hammering. "What did you know?"

"Everything," he replies. "I knew you would change every-thing. That you would be my everything."

Alistair strokes my cheek, kisses the corner of my top lip. I open my mouth and lick him, inviting him to kiss me deeply, to devour me.

My pussy tingles, eager for his cock. I can't believe after that immense fucking that I would crave more, but here we are.

Alistair puts bands on my wrists to protect them from further rope burn, then lashes them together to the headboard so that my hands are above my head. He takes a moment to admire my breasts, which are still glossy from the coconut oil massage. Then he loops the rope loosely around my ankles and back again to my wrists so that I'm trussed like a hunter's trophy, completely vulnerable. The tingling turns into a more active desire to be filled up by him.

"Is this okay?" he asks.

I nod. "Yes. But you don't need to check on me. I'll stop you if it becomes too much. I want you to do whatever you want to."

His eyes darken, and his expression grows hungrier still. I can almost feel his gaze biting into me. I wish he'd put his cock in my mouth.

Alistair looks at my lips and back into my eyes. He swipes my bottom lip with his thumb, not resting it long enough for me to suck it. He lifts my trussed ankles and ducks beneath the rope so that it's on the back of his neck while my feet are on either side of his face. I'm pretty much folded in half. It's a good thing I love yoga.

Alistair massages my breasts and tweaks my nipples. My craving grows.

"I love your tits," he growls, then sucks my nipples. "You're so fucking hot."

If the previous orgasm was like a fully lit-up Christmas tree, I can now feel the lights all coming on again one by one. Not that I'll climax again. It's impossible.

Alistair moves up to my neck and kisses me, then covers my eyes with his thumbs as he explores my mouth with his. My body starts moving beneath him, making its want known.

"Please don't make me wait," I say. I won't survive another foreplay marathon.

Alistair looks amused. "Yes, ma'am."

With that, he eases his magnificent cock into my swollen, sensitive, slick pussy.

I sigh deeply. "Ah! So good."

He draws in a hissing breath through clenched teeth. "Fuck, Ivy."

It's perfect, being filled up like this when I'm so alive inside, so switched on.

"Perfect," he says, as if he had read my thoughts.

I push everything out of my mind and focus on the intense pleasure I feel radiating through my body. The Christmas lights are all twinkling, and getting brighter.

He moves in and out exquisitely slowly, and my pleasure begins to arc again. I moan and whisper to him as he keeps going, keeps penetrating my swollen body, hitting the exact right spot. He knows my body better than I do.

Oh fuck, I can feel it coming. That rolling wave. My breathing changes, grows ragged. I try to breathe deeply, try to settle into the bliss, but my body has other plans.

"Ohhhhhh," I moan. "Ohhhhh fu-u-u-u-uck." I'm so close.

"Wait," says Alistair. "Wait."

I shake my head. "I can't. It's too late. It's too good."

He withdraws.

What? No! "Alistair!" I plead.

"You're going to have to wait," he says, looking like a Greek god again. Everything chiseled and tanned and ridiculously good-looking.

"No," I cry.

"It'll be worth it," he promises.

But I don't want to wait. I want that beautiful orgasm that was seconds away. I had already felt the beginning of the sparks. What could possibly be better than that?

He turns his face to kiss my foot. I think it will tickle, but it sends an arrow of longing all the way up my leg. Searing torment. Why is he torturing me?

"Okay," he finally says. "It's time."

CHAPTER 40

Sexual Alchemy

ALISTAIR

It takes every ounce of my willpower to wait, to give Ivy's body the time it needs to ramp up to the kind of orgasm I know she is now capable of. Every cell in my being wants to let loose and just pound her senseless, to just smash into her until she gets what she needs. But I know that if I am just a little more artful, I'll be able to give her the orgasm of a lifetime. I can tell her body is primed and ready. After what we have both been through these past weeks, this is what we need. I've always known that sex has the power to transform, but I've never felt it before. It's Ivy that makes sex transformative. She diminishes my trauma and takes away my pain. An hour in bed (or up against a wall) with Ivy is worth a dozen on a couch with a psychologist.

I remember being out of my mind with worry for Ariana when we found her—seeing all that blood puddling around her. The chopper ride was agony. Then, in that clinical hospital setting when Ariana was in the operating theatre, I was so scared that I felt like my thoughts were going to spin out of control, my sanity along with them. But Ivy took me aside and gave me what I needed to ground myself again. She lets me exorcise my demons through her —and her heart is so good that the demons just bounce off her. Or perhaps they don't ricochet, perhaps they transform into something else. Something pure, through the sexual alchemy of Ivy Mickelson.

Christopher would laugh if he could hear me. The man I was before meeting Ivy wouldn't entertain such thoughts. Ivy's concerned that *she* has changed, but I think I have changed the most.

Ivy's gazing at me, drunk with desire. The silky rope on the back of my neck reminds me of how close I came to dying, and that Ivy has given herself to me totally.

Ah, my cock is so hard; almost too hard. My balls are aching. We're locked in this surreal position, tied in golden knots. I take a breath. It's go time.

I reach for the small steel butt plug that I've been warming next to my leg under the cover. It's a luxury brand—and it looks it—with its sophisticated shape and elegant design. I slather it with lube, and when Ivy sees it, her eyes lose that dreamy look. She blinks and swallows. I give her a moment to stop me if she wants to, but she remains silent, only her body betrays her nervousness. Gauging by her reaction, I'm assuming she's never played with a plug before, so I'm glad that I chose the petite size.

Ivy swallows again. I can see she's scared, but she trusts me.

I press the slippery toy to her rim and swirl it around for a while, getting her used to the feeling and drawing out the anticipation for both of us, before slowly dipping just the tip.

"Ah!" she moans. Shock and delight. Her fingers clench into fists above her head. She's still looking at me: a deer in headlights.

I cup her mound, the heel of my hand pressing against her clit, keeping her safe and warm, then press the toy a little further into the tight muscle. She exclaims again and doesn't close her mouth. I feel a rush of blood to my cock, which is straining to get inside her. We breathe together, slowly, deeply, never breaking eye contact as I increase the pressure on her clit and push the plug into her asshole a fraction more. We're almost halfway in. Ivy bites her bottom lip, trying to control her fear and her pleasure.

I find it so erotic that I edge closer to my own climax.

I know that I won't last long.

I observe her face as I slowly—achingly slowly to enjoy every second—push the rest of the slick bulb inside her rim. Ivy gasps and arches in pleasure. Her mouth is still open, and her eyes roll back and close as she moans loudly. Fuck.

"Good girl," I murmur, stroking her, telling her with my warm skin and firm pressure that we are safe. She is still moaning as goosebumps spread up her arms and thighs.

First level of bliss unlocked, I move on to the grand finale. I grab more lube and rub it onto my greedy cock. It's so engorged that it's almost painful. Ivy's eyes are still closed, her body folded in half by mine. I place the tip at the entrance of her delectable pussy, which is still sensitive and wet, and she gasps again.

She probably thinks it'll be too much, but I know she can take it.

I need more lube. We are both so swollen that my cock feels too big.

I try again, and her eyes fly open. "It's not going to fit."

I smile. "It's going to fit."

"I'm not ready," she says.

"You are more than ready," I reply.

"Put it in my mouth first," she says. "Please. I want your cock so badly. I want it in my throat."

I shake my head. If my cock gets anywhere near her mouth it'll all be over.

"No," I say, and she accepts it. "I know you're scared, but you trust me, right?"

Ivy nods, still wide-eyed. I add more lube and try again, easing the tip of my cock inside. We both moan with the intense pleasure of it. So fucking tight and juicy.

"Fuck, Ivy." I'm about to explode. I breathe slowly to keep it together, but just seeing the base of the plug in her ass makes me crazy with desire. Her moaning lips, bouncing tits, juicy pussy ... it's almost too much to handle when I'm so ready to detonate.

Breathe, I tell myself. *Breathe, you lucky bastard.*

"I need you," I tell her. "I need this."

Ivy nods. "Take me," she whispers. "I'm ready. I want you deep inside."

I take another breath, then force my rock-hard shaft into her. It's so compact I gasp.

She yells in surprise and pleasure. Her voice high and breaking when she says "Fuck!"

I watch her face, her expression hot and blissed out, and as I begin to rock into her she looks like she'll weep. I'm about to ask if she's okay when she cries out and whimpers "Yes-yes-yes-yes."

I breathe and keep rocking, feeling the beginnings of my orgasm rushing through me, ready to erupt.

Not yet, not yet, not yet.

This is too good to stop. This is everything.

Ivy cries out again and keeps whimpering and nodding. I didn't think it could get any more intense, but then her fluttering muscles clench my cock and I almost come. I pause for a moment, watching Ivy's rapture.

"You're so beautiful, Ivy," I grind out. "You feel so good. You're the best thing that has ever happened to me. I want to fuck you all day."

I know it will be a potent release for her if this orgasm makes her cry. It's already been a powerful balm to my state of mind, being able to penetrate her like this, like nothing else matters.

I mentally prepare myself to double down without coming too soon.

"You're ready," I tell Ivy. It's not a question.

She bites her lip and nods, golden-trussed fists clenched. I hold her wrists against the headboard, giving me the leverage I need, then thrust into her as hard as I can. She yells and whimpers. I know I'm hitting all the right places —it's like we're perfectly melded together. Made for each other. I thrust again, then again, Ivy's cries getting shriller as I increase my pace. Soon my body is crashing into hers, hard and fast, almost out of control. I lift her hips slightly so that my thrusting body hits up against the plug every time I drive into her.

Double penetration. Harder. Faster.

Ivy screams as her orgasm hits her. Her muscles spasm around my cock, and I know it's over. I fuck hard into her orgasm, making it more intense, making it last longer. I thrust until I can't anymore, until my whole body feels like it's going to spiral out of control.

"Still coming," she sobs, muscles spasming.

It's my turn to yell as I drive into her one last time, her pussy strangling my cock. I explode into a galaxy of bliss: darkness and stars and this woman who gives me everything.

CHAPTER 41
Romantic AF

IVY

Holy, holy, holy shit.

I'm sobbing in Alistair's arms. He untied me and rained kisses on my face, then scooped me up into his arms. Now he's holding me tight, breathing into my tousled hair, brushing away the tears. Murmuring that I'm beautiful, that I'm everything, that he'll never be able to love someone like he loves me. I'm so blissed out that I can hardly move.

I want the record to reflect that I have never, EVER had an orgasm as intense as that. Climaxes before I met Alistair were like sneezes compared to this. It's unmoored me, knowing that sex can be this incredibly intense; so utterly intoxicating. How am I supposed to keep living an ordinary life after I have experienced this?

The crying was unexpected, but I felt the tension and grief draining from my body as they flowed. It's like Alistair fucked the bad experiences away, fucked them into oblivion. Jeff Bates no longer holds any power over me. He is well and truly gone. Alistair has healed me.

His new phone rings, causing us both to frown.

Alistair kisses me and stretches for it. After looking at the caller ID, he answers.

"Henderson?"

"Heard a scream, Sir."

Alistair catches my eye, and we hold back a naughty laugh.

He clears his throat. "Yes," he replies. "You heard correctly. Everything's fine here."

I'm biting my lips to stop from giggling.

"Just checking."

"You're a good man, Henderson. See you tomorrow."

"Yes, Sir."

Alistair ends the call and rolls into me, kissing me as I laugh.

"Poor Henderson," I say. "Does the man ever sleep?"

"Never seen it," replies Alistair.

We lie cuddled up for a while, enjoying the last pulses of pleasure shooting through our bodies, the fizzling out of the final sparks.

"That was … incredible," I venture. Even the word "incredible" doesn't seem to do it justice. "Sorry about the crying."

"Oh, you must never apologize for tears, Ivy," he says softly, stroking my arm.

"It just felt … it felt like you reached deep inside me and … fixed something."

"Yes," he pulls me even closer. "I feel the same. You fix me."

"We fix each other," I reply.

I'm sure Becks would label it as an unhealthy co-dependent thing to say, but I'm not sure I give a damn. It's true, and it's romantic as fuck.

I look into Alistair's eyes.

We fix each other.

The morning sun blasts us out of bed. It's a good thing, too, because we had slept like hibernating mammals, long and deep, and we had an hour to get to the beach party we were supposedly hosting.

"It's all taken care of," Alistair assures me, stopping me from wringing my hands.

Of course, when you're swimming in hundreds of millions of pounds sterling, you never have to lift a finger, even if you are the host.

"You must be looking forward to seeing your family," I say.

"I am," he replies, pulling on a soft linen collared shirt that makes him look relaxed and ridiculously handsome. "But I'd rather spend the day in bed with you."

I cackle. "You're crazy," I say, although I don't mean it. "After that ultra-shagathon!"

"*Shag*-athon?" he laughs. "Is this an Austen Powers movie?"

"Don't pretend you've watched Austen Powers."

"I haven't," he admits. "But I've seen the memes."

I wiggle my eyebrows at him and put on an accent. "That's groovy, baby."

Alistair shakes his head at me being cheesy. He loves me.

"I'm glad we're having a party," I say. "What shall I wear?"

"As little as possible," he replies.

"Ha, ha."

"A party dress," he says. "We have a lot to celebrate."

"You being alive, for one."

"Indeed. We also need to celebrate the earth-shattering sex we had last night."

"This is true," I agree. "It was certainly a lifetime highlight for me."

"I'm sure my family will be happy to hear it."

I throw a pillow at him. He catches it easily and makes the bed.

We have a quick coffee and a pastry out by the pool while we wait for Henderson to collect us.

"You look fucking gorgeous," Alistair says, looking me up and down.

"That's because you're still all full of happy sex hormones," I reply.

"That may be true, but the fact remains."

I'm wearing a simple long white flowing dress cinched with a leather belt under my bust.

He's still staring. "You look so ... *pure.*"

"You know what they say," I tell him with a smirk. "Looks can be deceiving."

In the car on the quick journey to the beach, Alistair takes my hand. "A lot has happened since that night on the yacht."

"That's putting it mildly," I reply.

"What I mean to say is that I haven't forgotten about our discussion. About you starting and heading up the charity foundation at the company."

My anxiety spikes. *Oh yes, that.*

"Er," I hesitate, looking out of the window.

Alistair's brow furrows. "You've ... changed your mind?"

"No!" I insist. "I just ... I was feeling on top of the world. Confident. Powerful, even."

"I like that," replies Alistair.

"I was drunk on warm weather and orgasms and Thai cocktails."

"I like that, too," he murmurs.

"In the cold light of day, however ... I'm not sure I'm brave enough."

Alistair scoffs. "You? Not brave enough? You must be joking. You have every quality required—and more—to make a huge success of this. You're the perfect person for the job. My only regret is that I didn't think of it first."

"But I have zero experience. I don't know how to run the books. I'm completely unqualified. I'll probably make some awful mistakes and cost the company millions. And as soon as your family realize, they'll fire me. Which will make Sunday lunches awkward."

Alistair takes a deep breath and sighs it out. "First of all, you don't need experience. And you certainly don't need accounting skills—we have people for that. You will make mistakes, as we all do, and they will be swiftly forgiven and forgotten. Regarding Sunday lunches, you have nothing to worry about as they are, as you know, already supremely awkward. Anything else?"

I tap my foot, not sure what else I can say.

"It's normal to be nervous. You've never been in corporate before."

"Ugh. That's another thing. Corporate clothes and working in an office. It's just not me."

"There's the protesting hippie I know and love," chuckles Alistair. "You won't need an office in London. I mean, you're welcome to one, but as far as I'm concerned, you can work from home in your pajamas. Reacher and Bijou will be thrilled. Or, even better, work by the pool in your bikini—then I'll be the one who'll be thrilled."

I smack his shoulder.

"What?" he demands. "Imagine all the people you can help. You'll improve *my* life immensely just by lounging around in said bikini."

"You're just indulging me," I say. "Even if this was a terrible idea, you'd still encourage me."

"I don't know about that. But the truth is that our charitable efforts are ad hoc and not nearly as effective as they could be. So, really, you'd be helping my family *and* the people who need it."

If I don't completely fuck it up, I think to myself.

"Besides," he continues. "We're going to need all the help we can get to successfully navigate steering the company into ... legal waters. The PR points we'll gain through the work of the foundation will go far, especially as we'll need to find new clients to make up the shortfall."

"You're saying *I'll* be playing a part in cleaning up Ravenscroft Enterprises?"

"That is exactly what I'm saying. It'll be a hell of a lot more effective than standing outside with a placard, singing Bob Marley resistance songs. You're basically getting exactly what you asked for that day—an opportunity to change the world for the better.”

I look into his intense eyes. God, I love this man.

A smile plays on his lips. “You forget that I know you, Ivy Mickelson. I know you inside and out.” He squeezes my hand. “If anyone can do this, it’s you.”

CHAPTER 42

Bonfire & Rum

ALISTAIR

Walking across the beach toward my beaming family with Ivy on my arm and Henderson beside me is a wonderful feeling. I'm a different man, living a life unrecognizable from before.

"Alistair!" shout Mother and Brumilde in chorus.

There are paper lanterns and fairy lights strung all around, and the table is set beautifully. The soft sand beneath us and the ocean in the background is just perfect. I make a mental note to tip the party planner generously.

Clinging happily to Brumilde is baby Alex, who I see for the first time through a lens finally untainted by guilt. The warm feeling in my chest grows warmer still. Father and Christopher raise their glasses to me, smiling. We reach them quickly and exchange hugs, greetings, and admonishments. I get told off for giving them such a fright, and for making them wait so long to see me. Ivy gets scolded for keeping me to herself, and Christopher gets into trouble for already having polished off a bottle of Pinot Noir. Even the baby is tut-tutted for growing too quickly and being too cute, which he fully deserves.

"Ah, this wonderful!" exclaims Mother. "Isn't this just wonderful?"

We all nod and laugh and sit down to drink in earnest. It's been that kind of week.

I glance at two empty chairs at the table, not knowing who they could be for. All the Ravens are accounted for. Ivy's shriek alerts me to the newcomers, and she jumps up to hug her friend Rebecca, who seems to have brought a plus-one. I give Henderson an uncertain look, but he nods and gives me a subtle thumbs-up. I assume Brodie has done the relevant background check and approved the invitation. I'm not wild about having to share this special event with a stranger, but Ivy has her best friend here, and I can't complain about that. I tell Henderson to grab an extra chair as I push a cold bottle of lager into his hand.

"You're off-duty for the next twenty-four hours," I instruct him.

He would argue, except he knows it would be fruitless. This is a family affair, he's family, I'm the boss, and we have plenty of bodyguards between the lot of us.

A waiter brings us piña coladas, margaritas, and other frothy concoctions, mostly of the rum and coconut variety.

The bonfire to the east of us is lit, and we all cheer as the flames race up the teepee of kindling.

"Fire has a purifying effect, I find," says the stranger. "Always good for a new chapter. I'm Noah." He sticks out his hand, and I shake it.

"Alistair," I reply. "Welcome to the party."

Henderson side-eyes the guest, but now that Brodie had cleared the man, I suspect it might have more to do with the fact that he's had his eyes on Rebecca rather than seeing Noah as a physical threat. Ivy's in her element, throwing back cocktails and laughing with her best friend. I take Alex from Brumilde and pop him on my lap. I give him a piece of pineapple to try. He screws up his face at the tartness of the fruit but immediately wants more. Everyone watching him laughs. After he's had his fill, I turn him around so that his little body rests against me. The distribution of his weight changes, making me think he's falling asleep despite the rowdiness of the company.

"I used to be like that," says my brother.

"Lies. You've never been this cute in your life," I tell him.

He pouts at me. "What I meant was, I used to be able to sleep anywhere."

"Nothing's changed, then," I reply.

He concedes with a smirk and takes a sip of his lethal-looking cocktail.

I can smell the burning wood, the salt water, the lemon-grass. I inhale deeply, trying to get it all in, trying to fix this moment in my memory forever. Ivy guffaws at my side. Everything is perfect.

The waiters bring hot chicken broth spicy with chili and galangal. They serve prawns wrapped in rice pastry, deep-fried and slathered in sweet chili sauce, and sweet corn cakes with fresh coriander and lime salt.

"These are the starters," says Mother, looking at Christopher, who has already hoovered up a fair share of the food. "Save some space for the main course."

"Oh, *Smother*," he says fondly. "You do know that I'm thirty-ish years old, right? I *do* have a mild grasp of how to survive in the wilderness without your … *constant* guidance."

I snigger at the "wilderness" part and earn a sharp glance from Mother.

"It's a wonder, really," she mumbles.

"That I've survived so long as an adult?" Christopher asks.

"That I haven't disowned you yet," she replies, and everyone chuckles.

Brumilde doesn't join in the banter, but she looks content, sitting back and seeing us all together.

"What's this thirty-ish business?" I ask. "Does too much rum make you forget your actual age?"

Christopher sighs in mock fatigue, then polishes his already-buffed fingernails on the front of his shirt. He admires them, then looks up at Alistair and shrugs casually.

"It's the new thing. No one has to know your exact age, right? And there are different ways to count your years, anyway."

I snort. "No, there are not."

"He's right," says Mother—which may be a first. "My watch tells me that my biological age is fifty-five."

"Your biological age?" I drawl. "As opposed to your—?"

"Chronological age," says Christopher.

"Now I've heard it all," laughs Father.

I look at him, surprised and grateful that he is well enough to be with us. "You're looking good."

He guffaws again. "Don't tell me I look like I'm forty-ish, because I won't bloody believe you."

We all laugh, more with relief than anything else.

Still holding the sleeping Alex on my lap, I let out a big sigh and squeeze Ivy's knee. She awards me with a blinding grin. I feel the warmth of the bonfire and rum. I feel like the weight I've been carrying for so long has finally lifted off my shoulders.

CHAPTER 43

The Jungle

IVY

I'm living my very best life. The food is delicious, the setting glorious, and I get to sit with the love of my life on one side and my BFF on the other. Bonfire blazing, cocktails on tap, and, best of all, we're all together and we're safe. I realize that I haven't felt safe in years.

Growing up in my parents' home was a privilege. We'd never been wealthy, but we had all the love we could ever want. Most of the time it felt safe, but Jamie's health was always up in the air. Every time my baby brother seemed to be doing well, he'd have some kind of medical scare that would pull us under a heavy cloak of overwhelming anxiety and grief. Knowing that Jamie may not survive another night in hospital, attached to all the beeping and pumping machines used to terrify me. It often felt like a happy, normal life was just out of my grasp.

As Jamie matured, his health grew more robust, and the scares became less frequent. The cold fingers of fear constantly wrapped around my heart released their grip, only to return when Jeff Bates entered my life, and more panic—and shame, and guilt—ensued. When Alistair went missing last week, all the terror came flooding back, so much so that I thought I would go mad. All of this is to say that I do not take this golden time for granted, but I do find myself relaxing into it, because I know how fleeting it can be.

The waiters bring grilled chicken satays with peanut sauce, beef satays in spicy plum, and platters of *Miang Kham,* fresh raw one-bite spinach parcels with coconut, lemongrass, and cashews. Christopher surveys the raw spinach with distaste. He stops the waiter from putting the plate down, points at me, and mouths *vegan,* so I get an extra helping.

"How incredible is this food?" demands Becks, wiping a drop of sauce off her chin.

"Definitely a step up from our regular Asian food," I reply.

She gives me a mock-frown. "Don't you talk trash about our fave Chinese! That place is an institution." She turns to Noah. "Ivy and I always go to this cheap and cheerful hole in the wall in Chinatown. We eat ramen and drink all the sake we can afford."

"And have the deepest conversations," I add.

"I'd love to be a fly on the wall," replies Noah.

Nostalgia makes me sigh. "We should go back. For old times' sake."

Becks nods. "I'm in!"

I turn to face Alistair, who still has Alex on his lap. "You're not eating?"

Alistair smiles and looks down at the sleeping infant. "Don't want to drop food on the baby."

I laugh and put out my arms. "You're hogging him. Let me hold him for a while, and you can eat."

I was going to make a joke about him needing his strength for later, wink-wink, but something stops me. Maybe it's the fact that he's still looking a bit on the thin side after his ordeal. All the more reason for him to eat, but I don't want to be the one to remind him of what he's been through.

Alistair passes me the slumbering bundle, and I hold him against my chest. He makes a couple of snuffling noises as he settles against me, then relaxes completely as he falls back to sleep. I love the feeling of his small warm body up against mine, the scent of his hair, and the feel of his cozy pajama onesie. God, could this moment be any more perfect?

Alistair makes short work of the food on his plate. Isobel stands, holding an elegant glass, and we stop talking amongst ourselves to listen.

"Dear beloved boy," she says, looking at her firstborn. "Thank GOD you returned safely."

"Since when do we believe in God?" chirps Christopher.

Isobel catches my eye. "Ivy, darling, do me a quick favor and kick Christopher in the shins."

"Ouch!" Christopher yells, gaping at me. "That was sore!"

I roll my eyes. Even if I wanted to kick him, I wouldn't be able to reach with Alex on my lap.

"Thank you," says Isobel, a youthful mischief in her eyes.

"I'll keep it short. I have to, because I promised myself that I wouldn't cry." She swallows and continues. "Alistair. We are so very grateful to have you back, and all in one piece."

There is some murmuring around the table, most likely regarding the dismembered ear we were sent in the black ribboned gift box. Fucking Russians. I hold Alex closer.

"As I said, I'm not going to make a long speech. I think we're all emotionally exhausted. I just wanted to say, Ravens, I love you all, and I'm proud of you."

"Proud of Christopher?" Alistair teases. "That's a first."

"Hey!" Yells his brother. "I won the egg-and-spoon race in grade 2!"

We all laugh, probably less at Christopher's wit than just the bubbly, happy feeling we all share—and the rum in our veins.

"Cheers," says Isobel, raising her glass.

We do the same, and chink glasses. When Isobel sits down, I see Gregory pat her shoulder and nod vigorously. *Good speech, darling,* I can imagine him saying. *Very good.*

The waiters clear the table, topping up drinks and replacing the dinner platters with dozens of candles that flicker in the breeze. They light bamboo torches along the beach as far as the eye can see.

Faces turn to look at Alistair, so he clears his throat and stands up.

"I haven't prepared anything," he says. "Given the location, I erroneously assumed the party would be a relaxed affair with no formal program."

We chuckle.

"It's a Ravenscroft function," says Christopher. "It goes without saying. I'm surprised Mother didn't order us to wear tuxedos. Or, at the very least, our smoking jackets."

Brumilde shakes her head ruefully and tsk-tsks Christopher. How she coped when she was their nanny, I'll never know. There is, always, affection in her eyes.

Alistair indulges his brother with a smile. "I do, however, have a couple of things to say."

We stop tittering and pay attention. I'm sure Alistair has always known how to command a room, or in this case, a luxurious table on a beach, with the paper lanterns bobbing in the warm breeze, and waves lapping at the shore.

"Without making too much of it, I would like to take this opportunity to reiterate my intention to clean up our operations within the corporation."

"Not this again," groans Christopher.

Alistair presses ahead. "If this experience has taught me anything, it's that the safety of our family is paramount."

I feel a new warmth spreading in my chest. I couldn't possibly love him any more.

"You can't wrap us all in cotton wool," argues his brother, which makes me really want to kick his shins. "It's always been a jungle out there. And we know how to operate in the jungle. That's our edge over our competitors. That's why we're so fuck-off successful."

"Language," cautions Isobel.

"I understand what you're saying," Alistair replies carefully. "We did what we needed to grow the business and the family fortune. We were good at it."

Christopher pretends to clear his throat and whispers "Understatement!"

Alistair ignores him. "But now that we have what we worked for, what we risked our lives for, we no longer need to operate in the danger zone. In fact, it would be foolish because in doing so we'll risk losing everything we've accomplished."

There's my Alistair, mitigating risk all over the place. My heart.

"It's time to switch off our autopilot and actually think about what we want for ourselves, for the business, for the family. Our aim is not to be rich beyond measure—"

"Speak for yourself," chirps Christopher, but not in an unkind way. He does understand, even if he doesn't like it.

"There are many different kinds of wealth," Alistair says. "We've always had it in this family. And I have found a new kind with Ivy."

I blush under his gaze and rub Alex's back. Isobel is blinking away tears. I look around for a tissue, certain that I'll be crying, too. Becks notices and takes the baby from me, letting him snuggle against her for a while. Watching them, Noah gets a dreamy look in his eyes.

"Loves kids," whispers Becks. "He's a nightmare."

I look back at Alistair with so much love, and find him returning my gaze.

"And I don't ever want her, or anyone else in this family, to be in danger again. I'll do what I can to protect you all. My top priority going forward in Ravenscroft Enterprises will be to legalize all the operations we can, and wind up the ones we can't."

"Hear, hear," says Gregory, and lifts his glass, which makes us all stare. We recover quickly and lift our drinks to join him.

Even Christopher reluctantly does his part. "To the new chapter in Ravenscroft Enterprises!"

It seems surreal that they're agreeing, and I'm certain there will be many stumbling blocks ahead, but I'll take the small wins along the way.

CHAPTER 44
Scuffed Velvet

ALISTAIR

We are surrounded by the flickering warm light from the dozens of candles and beach torches, while the bonfire burns fiercely in our midst. We are all light-headed, light-hearted, warmed by fire and rum.

The live band start setting up, signaling that dinner is over and the party will start soon. The band members have their traditional instruments, and the lead vocal, a beautiful woman in an emerald silk dress, sways to the rhythm, preparing to sing.

"One more thing," I say, still standing. "Just a minor detail."

My family looks at me, perhaps expecting a housekeeping memo, like what time the jet will be leaving in the morning to take us home. They're distracted, tipsy, and ready to dance. Christopher is eyeing not one, but two of the waitresses, and Father's eyelids look heavy. Noah is playing peek-a-boo with Alex, who is now awake and gurgling with delight.

Henderson and Ivy are the only ones who look vaguely interested in what I'm about to say, Ivy smiling at me, misty-eyed. Probably—hopefully—thinking of last night's incredible orgasm.

I clear my throat loudly and that seems to get everyone's attention.

"While I was locked away, things were surreal and hazy." Now everyone is focused, hanging on to my every word. "But as the time passed, I gained clarity. Not only about where I was and what I had to do to stay alive ... it also became clear to me what matters most in life, and that's the people in it."

Mother's eyes sparkle with tears. Brumilde hunts for tissues.

"Who are you and what have you done with the real Alistair?" jokes Christopher.

I smile at him. "My life's mission became clear to me. I'll do everything I can to protect you all, no matter what, and to make the most out of lives together."

Father seems to have perked up and is nodding vigorously.

I could swear that I'm not nervous, but my heart decides otherwise and starts hammering against my ribs.

"And so I thought ... what better time to commit to you all, and also offer my commitment to Ivy."

Eyes widen, spines straighten.

I reach into my pocket for the little gift I had brought home. A hinged box covered in scuffed velvet.

I smile nervously at Ivy, her expression vacillating between joy and terror. I take her hand and pull her up to stand before me, my nerves jangling.

"Ivy Mickelson. In the short time I've known you, you've turned my life upside-down. You completely wrecked the status quo."

There is nervous chuckling around the table.

"I was living in a cold, dark corner, and you've lit it up with your sunshine. I've never been happier or more fulfilled, and I have a feeling this is just the beginning."

Ivy's grinning now—thank god—as she nods at me. I breathe a little easier.

Okay. She knows what's happening and she's going to say yes.

"Now, before I open this box," I show it to her in the palm of my hand. "I must apologize that it's not up to our ... usual standards. It was the best I could get from the pawn shop on the way home."

Rebecca shrieks with delight, making Alex—wanting to share in the excitement—bounce on Noah's lap.

"You *didn't*," Mother scolds, appearing scandalized. "Not from a *pawn shop*."

"I did," I tell her. "I swapped the handgun I took off my captor."

"That might be the most romantic damn thing I've ever heard," says Christopher. Brumilde tosses her napkin at him. He catches it and winks at her.

Ivy's laughing gleefully at how my rude family is interrupting my very important proposal. I guess she understands that if she marries me, she will marry my absurdly dysfunctional family, too.

I open the box so Ivy can see the simple ring with its tiny, unpretentious sapphire. Her smile is so wide that you'd swear the ring was worth a million pounds.

I get down on one knee, my heart swelling.

"Beloved Ivy," I start.

I can't help thinking, but not saying out loud: *My pet, my mistress, my whore, my goddess.*

"It's not an exaggeration to say that I love you more than life itself. I can't imagine being without you. You'd make me the happiest man on earth if you agreed to be my wife. Will you marry me?"

Ivy, still grinning ear to ear, says "Only on one condition."

CHAPTER 45
Monkey~Face

IVY

I draw it out a bit, just for fun. Of course I'll marry Alistair. There will never be anyone else—mostly because he's ruined all other men for me. Is my heart practically beating out of my chest? Yes, yes it is. But I think it's got more to do with the fact that I wasn't expecting a marriage proposal any time soon. It's so early in our relationship, and I feel so young and naïve, but when it comes down to it, of course we'll be married. We've always known that we were meant to be together.

Alistair is still down on one knee. "Is your condition ... a nicer ring?"

I laugh and shake my head. "No. I love the ring. It's perfect."

Isobel frowns at me, and I'm sure she's thinking *we can't have that.* Or maybe she's wondering what my condition is.

I haul Alistair up. "I love you, Alistair Ravenscroft, and I'd love to be your wife. But I'd love it even more if we could adopt Alex as our son."

Everyone murmurs, and Brumilde outright sobs. A happy sob, I hope.

"OMG!" whispers Becks to the baby, who is now on Noah's lap. "Baby! Did you hear that? Did you hear what your new mama said?"

Alex chuckles at her crazy eyes.

Alistair gives me a thousand-megawatt smile and slips the ring onto my waiting finger. The fit is perfect. He grabs me, pulling me into a full-body hug that leaves me breathless. I feel every bit of him against me, and it's the very best moment of my life.

Or, perhaps the best moment of my life, I correct myself, *apart from the sex the night before.*

The band starts playing, and a bottle of tequila is placed on the table.

Christopher whoops and bangs the tabletop, the women cheer and queue to hug me, and Noah congratulates me and—rather reluctantly—hands over Alex for a giant hug. What can I say, I'm starting to like the guy.

"Hello monkey-face," I say to the baby. "Do you know that you're going to be *my* monkey-face soon?"

"This is the best news ever," beams Brumilde through her tears.

"It wouldn't have happened without you, Mildew," I say, using Christopher's nickname for her.

"Nonsense," she replies.

"It's true. I wouldn't be brave enough to do it on my own. But you're so experienced—and kind and wonderful—that I know it'll all work out."

She sniffs and puts her arms out for Alex. "Speaking of which, he'll need a bottle now."

I make wide eyes at her. "You see what I mean?"

Isobel kisses me on both cheeks and hugs me. "Welcome to the family, darling. I couldn't be more thrilled."

If you had told me a month ago that Mrs Ravenscroft would be thrilled at the prospect of having me as a daughter-in-law, I would have laughed—very loudly.

"You don't mind that he's marrying me and not some ... aristocratic heiress who went to finishing school?"

"Good god, darling, that sounds like nothing but a recipe for misery. You two are *perfect* for each other, as you very well know. And don't think I've forgotten how you saved my daughter's life. You are an asset to this family—and infinitely more respected than an insipid and spoilt princess from Fettes."

I'm trying to think of a reply when Gregory joins his wife's side.

"I thin kit might be time to call it a night, dear," he says.

"Of course, darling," Isobel replies, winking at me. *Don't take it personally,* the wink says. *He doesn't really understand.*

"Aren't you going to congratulate our young Ivy here?" prompts Isobel.

Gregory lifts his chin and surveys me with narrowed eyes. "Ah, yes, the food was delicious. Talented beyond measure, you are. Much appreciated."

He must think I cooked it. Probably due to our first ever conversation when we discussed Crêpe Suzette's use of white pepper in the Yorkshire puddings.

"You're very welcome," I reply, and return Isobel's wink.

Becks is next, wearing her most excited smile—an awkward grimace-like grin that always makes me laugh. Instead of a hug, I get a punch in the arm. "You could have bloody warned me!"

"I didn't know!" I reply. "I swear."

She sighs. "Ah, well, so much for me extricating you from all this."

"Was that your plan?" I ask. "To extricate me?"

"More of a recurring thought than a solid plan, if I'm honest."

"I'm glad you failed," I reply. "Because otherwise, I wouldn't have had *the best sex of my life* last night."

Someone behind me clears his throat. I turn and see Christopher opening his arms to me. Becks and I giggle like schoolgirls. Hopefully my blushing is hidden by my fire-warmed face.

"Come here, sis," he says, and gives me a bear hug. "Congratulations."

I wait for the inevitable vegan dig, but it does not come—probably because he's looking over my shoulder at the waitresses he was eyeing out earlier.

Henderson, ever formal, shakes my hand. "I'm happy for you both."

Alistair is back, and thumps Henderson on the back. "You're not drinking enough," he says. "Time to let your hair down."

"Yes, Sir," replies the bodyguard, and does no such thing.

CHAPTER 46

Deranged by Desire

ALISTAIR

"My beautiful wife-to-be," I drawl, offering Ivy my arm. "The grown-ups have left, and there's a bottle of very good tequila open. Do you fancy a drink and a dance?"

We shoot a glass with lime and salt, and then kiss each other and laugh, and dance at the bonfire. The band's playing a weird Thai version of the rock classics we know and love. It's perfect.

"Did you really trade a gun for this ring?" Ivy asks.

I nod. "It was a good piece, too. Solid and durable. It was also sentimental because I took it off Anya. I'm rather regretting trading it in, to be honest."

Ivy laughs and smacks my chest. "I have a feeling this isn't the last I'll hear of it."

I smile. "Every time we get into an argument I'm going to be thinking that I should have stayed away from that cursed pawn shop."

She rolls her eyes. "It'll be a running joke in your family for years. I can just imagine a drunken Christopher at Christmas yelling *'Should have kept the Makarov!'*"

"Oh, god," I laugh. "Perhaps I should have kept that part of the story to myself."

"Nah," she says. "Much more interesting this way."

I stop smiling for a moment. "You're sure you're ready? About Alex, I mean?"

"I'm not ready, but I'm going to do my best. He's the sweetest child, and he deserves a happy home. I want to be part of that. Besides, we'll have loads of help. Brumilde is a gem, plus Becks and Noah seem to be great with him—and that's saying something, because Becks usually abhors kids."

"Thank god for that," I say, "Because I don't have much faith in Christopher as a babysitter."

Ivy guffaws. "Never going to happen. No matter how desperate we are."

"Agreed."

She looks around. "Where is he, anyway? I expected him to be within arm's reach of the tequila."

"Probably snuck off with one of the hired help."

Ivy nods. "Sounds about right."

"Would ... *you* like to sneak off for a quick celebratory fuck?" I ask, raising my eyebrows.

She laughs. "We've been through this before. You are not capable of a quickie."

"Challenge accepted," I reply, and start dragging her off while she pretends to argue.

We find a dark copse and a floor of soft beach sand. I pick a tree that is smooth-barked and not laden with coconuts. I read once that coconuts kill more people than sharks. Imagine surviving the Russian Bratva only to be killed, mid-shag, by a coconut on the most important night of my life.

"Why are you smiling like that?" asks Ivy.

"Like what?"

"Like a deranged man."

In order to preserve the mood, I decide against mentioning killer sharks or their more murderous coconut counterparts.

"Because I have you."

"Having me makes you deranged?"

"A little, yes."

Deranged by desire.

I push Ivy up against the tree and kiss her. She still tastes like lime and salt, with a hint of tequila. I gently bite her lip while my hand lifts her dress.

"Mm," I moan. "I could kiss you all night."

"I'm afraid I'm going to need a little more than that," she replies, pressing into me so that she can feel my cock come to life.

I slip my hand into the front of her panties and stroke her beautiful pussy. "I can't believe you're mine."

"I was yours before the proposal," she replies, smoothing her hands over my muscles. "I've been yours since the moment you scooped me off that pavement. I thought you were a superhero, and then I realized you were a god."

I laugh into her neck. "I'm way too flawed to be either of those things."

"Not in my eyes," she whispers.

My fingers slip into the warm, wet part of her, and she moans. "I love the way you touch me."

My cock is fighting to get out of my pants. It strains painfully to be inside Ivy. She unbuckles my belt, unzips me, and holds it through the fabric of my boxers, making me groan and push against her hand like a teenage virgin.

"Quickies are fun," she says, breathing harder. "We should do it more often."

"I'm not happy unless you come. That's why I avoid them."

"I came long and hard enough last night to last me a life-time," she says. "Anything you do now is just a bonus."

I push my fingers further into her, and she moans again.

"In that case," I say, "You're in for a hell of a bonus. I'm going to make sure that you are the most well-fucked wife in the world."

CHAPTER 47
Skinny~dipping

IVY

The warm breeze, the effects of the tequila, a gorgeous man's magic fingers in my panties ... I'm thinking that this is the best beach party I've ever been to. I feel so young and free, like I want to pull off my clothes and go skinny-dipping in the sea. Alistair has other ideas. He pushes me against the tree, kissing me deeply as his hand brings a radiating warmth to my pussy. His fingers delve deeper, making me moan with pleasure.

"Promise me," I whisper.

He looks into my eyes. "Anything."

"Promise me we'll never stop having sex like this."

"Up against a palm tree?" he jokes.

I'm too horny to laugh. "Free, beautiful, boundless sex."

"That I can promise," he says.

He kisses me, his fingers moving deeper inside.

"But when we're married," I whisper. "And when we're parents. I don't want this to change."

"Our chemistry will never change," he growls. "I'll want you till the day I die."

I moan. "Tell me what you'll do to me."

"I'm going to fuck you every opportunity I get."

"Mm. What else?"

"We'll christen the rest of the manor, every room, and then we'll start again from the beginning. I'll eat you out on the kitchen counter. I'll bend you over the billiard table. I'll fuck you up against all the walls and in front of all the fireplaces."

His fingers are moving faster now, his thumb swiping my clit as he moves in and out. My pussy glows with pleasure and desire.

"What else?" I ask.

"We'll tick more boxes on our kink list, beginning with whichever turns you on the most. Starting first thing tomorrow and not stopping exploring till you've had your fill."

My breath is ragged. "I'll never have my fill."

"Then we'll get a new list. And a new one after that."

"What about parties?" I ask. "Play parties."

"I have an invitation sitting in my inbox. It's a fun one—a bit different. We'll be home just in time to attend. I think you're going to love it."

"I want to fuck another woman," I murmur, surprising myself. "And I want to watch you fuck her, too."

Alistair clears his throat. "That can certainly be arranged."

"And I want more of everything."

He bites my collarbone and fingers me deeper. "Can you be more ... specific?"

I moan and push against him. I'm so wet, and his touch feels so good. "More toys. More penetration. More playmates. More clubs like Iniquity. I want to try *everything*. I want it all."

"I want to give it all to you," he growls into my neck, increasing his pace.

"Fuck," I moan, as I feel my crescendo mounting. "I want you inside me now, when I come. I want to come all over your cock."

I take his shaft out of his boxers while he snaps my bra open. He nuzzles my breasts, the warm ocean air feeling good on my bare skin.

Magnificent cock in hand, Alistair's about to enter me when we hear a twig cracking underfoot. We freeze, hoping whoever it is will keep walking away from us. I rein in my heavy breathing so that we can hear. My carefree feeling fades. Are we in danger?

"Alistair?" comes a familiar voice. It's Henderson.

We don't move.

"You're not supposed to be on duty," replies Alistair.

"Sir. Permission to approach?"

"Wait there. I'll be right out," says Alistair.

We cover up, and I pull my fingers through my wild hair in an unsuccessful attempt to comb the tangles. Alistair takes my hand and we emerge from the dark, back to the flame-lit beach where Henderson, in his signature dark suit, cuts an anxious figure. He's holding his phone in a way that makes me think he's had some bad news—as if he's trying to put some distance between himself and the message he's just received.

"What is it?" Alistair asks. There is concern in his voice. He knows that Henderson would never interrupt him like this unless it couldn't wait.

Henderson rubs his forehead. "Jesus, Mary and Joseph."

That can't be good, I think.

"Brodie just called."

I have a sinking feeling in my stomach. Brodie never calls with good news.

"We need to leave immediately."

"Leave the party?" I ask.

"Leave the country," says Henderson. "I took the liberty. The jet's being prepared and the taxi is waiting."

"How bad is it?" asks Alistair, steeling himself for the news.

"There's no reason to panic, and no one has died," Henderson replies. "But we do need to get moving."

Alistair works it out quickly. "It's Ariana."

The bodyguard's lips are a thin line. He nods.

What has she done now? She was safe from our rival syndicate at the luxury rehabilitation center. I guess the one person she wasn't safe from was herself.

"She's escaped?" I ask.

"Worse," replies Henderson, wincing. "She's eloped."

～

THE END

After such a major cliffhanger in book 3, I couldn't do it to you again. Instead of writing the next ten chapters that would have ended in a HUGE cliffy, I held back.

So this book is shorter than I'd like, but I'll make it up to you in book 5 when a whole lot of action goes down.

I hope you'll join Ivy and Alistair's emotional rollercoaster that leads to their ultimate steamy HEA at the end of the series. At the moment it looks like book 6 will be the final book, but I'll only know for sure when I get there.

Thank you for your generous reviews of the series so far. And, most of all, thank you for coming along for the ride!

Mistress Blair

>> Order Book 5, Exploring All Things Bad here.<<
(pre-order delivery is scheduled for March 2025, but I'm hoping to publish it earlier)

>> Series page: Blood Money Billionaire <<

Also available in a paperback (books 1 - 4) and audiobook (books 1 and 2 so far. The rest is currently in production.) <3

I have some audiobook codes for book 1 to give away — so just shout if you'd like to listen.

I'm also considering a new-artwork limited edition

hardcover for the 6-book series. If you're interested, please let me know!

Janita

jtlawrence79@gmail.com

About Mistress Blair

Blair Butler is the steamy romance pen name of Kindle Unlimited All-Star and USA Today bestselling author JT Lawrence.

To be notified of new releases please join her Substack:

https://blairbutler.substack.com/

Shopify: www.jt-lawrence.com

Amazon author page: